Carl Weber Presents

Ride or Die Chick 1

Carl Weber Presents

Ride or Die Chick 1

J.M. Benjamin

www.urbanbooks.net

Urban Books, LLC
97 N18th Street
Wyandanch, NY 11798

Carl Weber Presents Ride or Die Chick 1 Copyright ©
2014 J.M. Benjamin

ISBN 13: 978-1-60162-610-3
ISBN 10: 1-60162-610-X

First Trade Paperback Printing April 2014
Printed in the United States of America

10 9 8 7 6 5 4 3 2 1

*This is a work of fiction. Any references or similarities
to actual events, real people, living or dead, or to real
locales are intended to give the novel a sense of reality.
Any similarity in other names, characters, places, and
incidents is entirely coincidental.*

Distributed by Kensington Publishing Corp.
Submit Wholesale Orders to:
Kensington Publishing Corp.
C/O Penguin Group (USA) Inc.
Attention: Order Processing
405 Murray Hill Parkway
East Rutherford, NJ 07073-2316
Phone: 1-800-526-0275
Fax: 1-800-227-9604

Carl Weber Presents

Ride or Die Chick 1

by

J.M. Benjamin

"Ride or Die Chick is the truth, truly one of the best books of 2014"

-Carl Weber

Prologue

"We now bring you live footage from Julie Sanchez of the actual chase. Hey Julie, what do you have for us?"

"Hello, Bob. As you can see, police are in a massive pursuit of a brand new, all-black 600 CLS Mercedes-Benz. Suspects are believed to be armed and dangerous. So far, all we know is that suspects entered onto Highway 264 westbound, coming off the ramp, headed toward the Virginia Beach area. It has been confirmed, Bob, that there are two occupants inside the vehicle, both African American—one male, the other female. Our sources who have been following the incident since it erupted, tell us that the driver has been identified as thirty-year-old Treacherous Freeman, from the Tidewater Park area in Norfolk, and thirty-year-old Teflon Jackson, from the Georgetown section of Chesapeake. Sources also say Ms. Jackson may have been injured at the actual scene. Though the actual count has not been confirmed, we are told that Mr. Freeman allegedly shot and possibly killed several officers and pedestrians during the horrendous gun battle, fleeing the scene of the crime while many others were wounded. The emergency medical team is tending those who were fortunate to have survived this unbelievable tragedy. As far as we know, no one was injured inside. Both Mr. Freeman and Ms. Jackson have criminal histories. Police authorities continue to pursue the two suspects, who seem as if they have no intentions on giving up at this time. We'll keep you updated as this tragic story continues to unfold here on Highway 264. This is Julie Sanchez, live from WAVY Ten. Back to you Bob."

"Thanks, Julie. Keep us posted. In other news, two teens were gunned down in the parking lot of a local McDonald's on Princess Ann Boulevard."

"Treach, I'm losing a lot of blood," cried Teflon as she applied pressure to the right side of her hip in an attempt to minimize the bleeding.

"Just hold on, boo, I got you. You gonna be a'ight. We gonna make it up outta this shit, and I'ma get you to a hospital," Treacherous assured his partner in crime as he navigated through traffic, switching lanes, weaving in and out with expertise, to elude the barrage of police cars that were on their trail. Treacherous cursed himself for not being able to foresee the predicament he was now faced with. All his life he had been trained, taught, and practiced being on point at all times. He had worked daily on perfecting the art of awareness and the ability to be alert. This time he had been careless and because of that, he had been put himself and Teflon in a compromising position. Now, his road dog was sitting across from him wounded, fighting for her life. Not only was Teflon his road dog, she was also his first and only love—his other half. Treacherous could not imagine losing her. The thought of it made him uneasy as he glanced over at her. He knew if he lost her, there would be no other reason for him to live. Before, they had freely discussed situations like the one they were faced with now, knowing in their line of work, death was a strong possibility. Because of their past preparation, they feared nothing in existence, so to them dying was not an issue. Still, Treacherous did not want things to end the way it seemed they would. He and Teflon promised each other if opportunity ever presented itself, they would both go together, so Treacherous was already preparing for the worst.

"Tef? Tef?"

"Huh?" Teflon answered in a low tone.

"Wake up, baby. Don't fall asleep. Stay awake, you hear me?" shouted Treacherous. He reached his hand over and began rubbing her silky hair.

"Daddy, I'm weak, and it's cold," Teflon moaned.

Treacherous had never seen his lady display this type of behavior before. In his eyes, she was as thorough as they came. Let him tell it, Teflon was the baddest female who ever walked the face of the earth. For her to show a sign of weakness now, even in her weakest state, was unacceptable. The whole sixteen years he had known her, from day one she carried herself as a trouper, so Treacherous refused to let her go out in any other way than that.

"Tef!" he barked, shaking her by the arm. "Man the fuck up. You a'ight. Shake that shit off. Stop all that mu'fuckin' whinin' and shit, and man the fuck up!" He accelerated on the gas pedal, noticing police cars gaining on them through the rearview mirror of the Benz.

His words poured into Teflon's almost lifeless body like a burst of energy and went straight to her heart. Just hearing her man's voice did something to her. Instantly, a sense of strength was breathed back into her. She had just about given up all hope of survival until Treacherous's voice had rejuvenated her. It was as though he had revived her with his firmness. Teflon smiled at Treacherous's tactics and was grateful for his intent. Since they had gotten together, Teflon had always felt she was the backbone. Though she was as strong as they came, whenever she was with him she felt equal in strength. But at times a sense of inferiority came over Teflon. Not to the point of being afraid, because Treacherous had never given her a reason to be. It was an inferior feeling only she as a woman could explain, because she was the only one besides God who even knew it existed. There were times in her life when she was with Treacherous and needed to feel like a woman and wanted to play her position as one in the presence of a man—her man, but she had never attempted to express this to Treacherous because she knew he viewed her as someone on the same level as himself, regardless of her gender and she didn't want to make him think any less of her. Treacherous was known throughout Virginia for not being the one to reckon with or cross. He was also known for having one of the hardest chicks in Virginia by his side, and Teflon wore and protected that title and reputation to the fullest, maintaining that facade, even behind closed doors with him, though she wished she could let her guard down. Now was one of those times where she felt that way, but it was not the time, so Teflon knew she had to put on her game face and suck it up.

"Who the fuck you yellin' at, boy?" Teflon managed to snap in a raspy tone. The strain caused her to choke.

Her cough alarmed Treacherous. He wondered if he should have come at her so strongly. In the past that's how they talked to each other, but things were different. He had never seen Teflon hurt before and the sight didn't sit well with him. He was glad to be hearing Teflon's voice despite her words that revealed her condition. Teflon sounded like her old self, but he knew she was in pain. The Teflon he knew and loved was stronger than the best of them. Treacherous felt she was tougher than all the men he knew put together, but still he didn't want to push her too much. After all, she was all he had in this world. With that in mind, Treacherous mentally vowed to see to it that she made it out of their situation in one piece, or at least he was prepared to die trying.

"Boo, my bad. Don't talk, save your strength," he said, moving Teflon's hair from out of her face. He noticed a trail of blood seeping out of her mouth and trickling down the side of her face. With his thumb he wiped what little he could.

"Don't start bitchin' up now, mu'fucka," Teflon shot back. Her tone was weak, but despite her condition she managed to smile.

Treacherous looked over at Teflon just in time to catch her smiling.

"Fuck you," he replied, revealing his own smile. As crazy and deranged as it may seem, for a brief minute, Treacherous and Teflon shared a Kodak moment. To anyone other than them it would have been considered an emotional scene between the two of them, but this was their normal behavior. It was the only way they knew how to express their affection for each other—or at least this was what they were used to. Treach blew the horn like a madman at the cars in front of him to clear the lane in hopes of getting an open stretch. He figured if he could just make it to Virginia Beach General Hospital, he and Teflon would be able to come up out of their situation alive. There was no doubt in his mind they would have to go back to jail—and for a long time for that matter—but at least they would still have each other. Treacherous had made a promise to himself a long time ago that he would never return back to confinement, but the fact that Teflon was dying made him reconsider. For a second he considered surrendering, turning himself over to the proper authorities if he got Teflon to the hospital, for her sake—if it meant saving his love's life, but just as quickly as it entered, it exited. He knew that Teflon would never agree to that. After all, she had made it perfectly clear that whatever happened to him happened to her. They were in this thing together until the bitter end. If it would have just been him then the notion would never had crossed his mind. Treacherous questioned whether he himself was becoming vulnerable due to his other half's current state.

He saw the sign up ahead for the Virginia Beach exit and maxed out the CLS speedometer.

"Boo, hold on. We almost there," he said as he approached the turnoff, but as he gazed over to look toward the passenger seat, he observed Teflon sitting there motionless, with her head tilted to the side, propped up against the window.

"Tef," he called again with the same results.

Instant rage overcame Treacherous as anger engulfed him. He could feel his blood beginning to boil. What he in fact tried to prevent had now come to pass, he thought. His other half, his better half, had been taken away from him. He was not in the least a God-fearing man because he was not brought up to be, so he cursed God for deciding it was Teflon's time. In Treacherous's eyes, she was too young and had been deprived of life too early. He could never recall a moment when tears were required because he had not been raised in such a way, so that emotion was foreign to him; still, he felt a sharpened pain in his heart and knew only Teflon could cause him such pain. He reflected on his past, when he had gone to visit his father for the first and only time in prison ten years ago. He had witnessed his father reveal his emotional side. His father had never done that before, and the sight of him in tears confused Treacherous. He couldn't understand why his father was displaying such weakness before him. He had always been portrayed in Treacherous's eyes as this emotionless, coldhearted gangsta. Treacherous was taught to believe gangstas didn't cry. Not on the surface, anyway. By believing that to be true, Treacherous began to see his father differently, once again, questioning his father's thoroughness. After that visit, he had never gone to see him again. There was no need to. In Treacherous's opinion, there was nothing else his father could tell him or teach him, for that matter, about being gangsta.

As he maniacally raced up 264, Treacherous began to shed a few tears. Not from the thought of his past, but for Teflon. Only his tears were internal. He cried gangsta tears.

Treacherous became filled with an indescribable pain, something he had never felt before for anyone else in the world. As his tears and rage intertwined inside of him, Treacherous made his decision. Without Teflon, there was no him. With that thought, he turned onto the exit ramp. Treacherous bought the CLS to a screeching halt just before reaching the end of the hospital exit.

When the FBI, DEA, SWAT, and state police saw the luxury sedan had come to a stop, they stopped along with it, leaving a thirty- yard distance in between them and the vehicle they had been pursuing for the past hour. Immediately, all of the participating officers and agents in the pursuit exited their vehicles with weapons drawn, finding position and coverage, expecting the unexpected, as the head agent in charge drew his bullhorn.

"Treacherous Freeman and Teflon Jackson, this is the FBI. You are under arrest. We need you to turn off the ignition to your vehicle, take the key out, and toss it out the driver's side window away from the vehicle, along with your weapons. Then slowly, I want you to open the vehicle doors one at a time, place your hands on top of your head, drop to your knees, and lay facedown flat on your stomach. You have three minutes to comply, do you understand? Three minutes," the head agent repeated.

Treacherous understood loud and clear, but had no intention of complying. To buy him some time, he took the two .38 revolvers he had tucked in his waist and threw them out of the driver's window along with the Benz keys, which he no longer needed. With the jet black–tinted windows on the Benz, it made it difficult, almost impossible, for them to see what he was doing. He then reached over and took Teflon's black .380 out of her lap and tossed it out the passenger's side.

Satisfied so far, thinking he had accomplished a great deal, seeing what he believed to be the weapons and the vehicle keys being thrown out of the windows, the head agent began to relax a little. He had been in this position many times, and the endings weren't always nice. He had been a negotiating agent for more than fifteen years and he had seen some of the most unnecessary outcomes in cases like the one he was negotiating now. The last thing he wanted to have happen was a shoot-out on a busy highway and wind up killing two troubled blacks, possibly getting both his men and innocent people hurt in the process.

After giving it some thought, he was confident that the outcome of this episode would be different.

"Very good, now slowly exit the vehicle, one at a time," he shouted into the bullhorn.

Treacherous laughed to himself at the naiveness of the agent.

Dumb mu'fuckas. All that training for nothing, he thought, referring to how easy it was to fool them. By now Treacherous had snatched up the two matching P-90 submachine guns with the see-through fifty-round clips on each side of the guns, which contained armor-piercing bullets. In total, he had two hundred rounds of cop killers in his possession, and intended to use them all. He took one last look over at Teflon, then leaned in, giving her a kiss on the lips. They were still a little warm.

"I love you, Tef," Treacherous spoke before he grabbed the door handle of the Mercedes- Benz.

Chapter One

"Ma'am. Push, push," the doctor requested.

"I am, goddammit," Teresa screamed back as Rich stood in the background with arms folded. He had a blank expression on his face. Rich was not ready to bring a child into a world that he felt was cruel and unjust, nor was he ready to become a father, but Teresa had insisted on having the baby. That being the case, Rich felt he owed her that much to stick by her once she told him of her decision, knowing all she had been through prior to and up until the time they had come back in contact with each other. Not including what she tolerated when it came to him. Teresa had been there for Rich through thick and thin, whether he wanted her to be or not, because she loved him.

Teresa Freeman fell hard for Richard Robinson, known as Richie Gunz, the first time they had met. The meeting was an awkward situation. Teresa was a good girl who was only attracted to bad boys. Being a redbone from Georgetown was like being Queen Elizabeth from England to all the pimps, players, and gangstas alike who were from not only Georgetown but from Norfolk, Hampton, Newport News, Portsmouth, and Virginia Beach as well. Teresa Freeman used that knowledge to her advantage to get some of the most major cats who ran the Virginia streets to pay attention to her. Although she was still a bona fide virgin, she was very much promiscuous for a seventeen-year-old, and every chance she got, she let it be known she still possessed her virginity, which only heightened men's attraction and lust for her tender-looking body. She stood every bit of five feet ten, possessing some of the smoothest-looking, long sunflower, complexioned legs ever introduced to mankind. They led up to a voluptuous heart-shaped apple bottom, followed by a petite waist that could be no more than a size twenty-eight, with a flat midsection to match, and a pair of marshmallow-soft 34C cups that stood at attention with grape-size nipples that protruded through her shirt. Even when she was braless her breasts stood at attention. Her lips were full, but her mouth was small. She possessed a sharp nose, with high cheekbones and a round face. Her eyes were quarter sized, not to mention gray, and they sparkled at the drop of a dime, making the strongest man melt. Teresa was definitely a sight to see coming through any area with her long, silky God-given, auburn-colored hair hanging down to the lower part of her back. Any man in his right mind would love to have a young trophy such as Teresa on his arm, and she knew it. What really attracted all the men to Teresa was the fact that she had come from a good pedigree: one of the best in Virginia.

Bo-Bo Freeman, who was Teresa's father, was one of the most vicious individuals from the Tidewater Park area, and her mother, Daphne Johnson, was what one would call a dime piece because of her all-around beauty, from the old school. She could still turn heads and put most of the young girls who thought they were hot stuff to shame, except for her daughter. Teresa was a fifty-cent piece. She was not only gorgeous; she was also a female gangsta at an early age. The way she carried herself was ladylike, but if you pissed her off or disrespected her in any way, then there was hell to pay. Teresa could transform in a split second from Dr. Jekyll to Ms. Hyde.

Teresa's father had been found executed in North Side Park when she was thirteen, and it had been her and her mother living together from that day until Teresa turned seventeen, when she let a major player put her up in her own apartment, paying her all expenses and rent for six months without her having to give him so much as a kiss, let alone sexual intercourse or fellatio. In the streets, one had to question who was actually the player and who was being played. Only a female of Teresa's caliber could have gotten something off like that on the man everyone referred to as Player Joe. At least that's what Teresa thought.

One day Teresa was returning back from a visit at her mother's house after a long lecture. Her mother cautioned her about being careful, due to the word on the streets that Teresa had Player Joe looking like a fool out in the public's eye. Being knowledgeable of the streets herself, Daphne knew the reputation of the young player her daughter was toying with was on the line, but she knew her words to her daughter had gone in one ear and out the other.

Teresa was glad to be up out her mom's house. Since she had been on her own, she and her moms had grown apart, but still she respected and loved her mother just the same and made it her business to pay her a visit once a week. It was the least she could do. As she reached the front of her one-bedroom studio apartment, she couldn't help but to think back to some of the things her mother had said, especially about Player Joe being the laughing-stock of the streets. She excused the thought and replaced it with her own logic, that if a man was going to be a sucka for a woman, then he deserved to be treated like one. That was one of the rules of the game and Teresa felt she was only playing by and respecting them. She smiled at her own theory as she searched for the key to the home she called her private castle. As Teresa fondled and rummaged through her Coach bag, she was so focused on finding her keys that she never saw the shadow that towered her or even knew what hit her.

   Rich, who was known as Richie Gunz for the twin trey-eight revolvers he toted and wouldn't hesitate to use, had just stepped out of Charlie's Bar admiring the redbone, when he saw an unidentified man step from around the car and attack the beautiful young girl, knocking her over the head with the butt end of his pistol. Rich had recognized the pretty girl when she first caught his attention. They had gone to school together—or rather they went to the same school because Rich was older. He remembered before he had dropped out to take on a full-time job as a number runner and a gun for hire, that she had been the prettiest girl in the entire school and was amazed at how she had maintained her beauty. At the time, Rich was in the sixth and she was in the fourth, but girls were the furthest thing from his mind back then. He was more focused on surviving and helping to take care of his mother. The sixth grade had been the extent of his education, textbook-wise anyway. Since then he had been getting his education through real life. Ever since Rich's mother had been murdered when he was fourteen, he had been out in the streets fending for himself.

   Although the girl named Teresa was still unmistakably gorgeous, that meant nothing to Rich and wouldn't justify him getting involved in something that didn't concern him. What did concern him, though, enough to make him aid the girl in distress, was the fact that his conscience would not allow him to witness a man putting his hands on a woman. That was something he was totally against. Rich had grown up seeing his father beat on his mother as if it were the normal thing to do for many years until he reached the age of twelve. One day he had taken all of his lunch money he had saved up and gone without eating at times, and bought him a .22 automatic. No sooner than he had made the purchase, Rich came home from school, in the midst of his dad beating up his mom—just like he anticipated—and he shot him in the chest six times, emptying the clip in him. His father lived, but never told the police what happened. That was the last time he and his mother had ever seen or heard from his father. Shortly after that, Rich became the man of the house and turned to the streets as a means of survival for him and his mother, becoming the new breadwinner of the household. Even then, Rich's mother still attracted the wrong type of men, who were physically and verbally abusive toward her. One by one, Rich would teach them lessons, that his mother was not a human punching bag, just as he had his father. Although Rich's mother was against him going out into the streets to make a living, she knew the part-time job she struggled to hold was not enough to cover even the rent of their two-bedroom apartment. Rich knew his father had been the one to bring the bacon home, paying all the bills, which was why he felt his mother had tolerated all of the abuse of those years, thinking she couldn't do better, that she and her child would be left out in the cold if she tried to leave him.

Rich felt it was only right to take on the responsibility as the man of the house and see to it that they were all right. Virginia streets were rough to be running, and Rich knew he had to get in where he fit in order to survive them. He began robbing, stealing, selling drugs, and running numbers, and it was all of that that put him in a position to tote two guns. Rich's theory was in the streets you had to keep both eyes open if you wanted to live, so why not carry two guns? It felt safer than just having one, he rationalized. Between running the streets and protecting his mother, guns were a necessity in his life.

Seeing the unfamiliar man take advantage of the pretty girl stirred up memories in Rich's mind of his mother. It disturbed him to see the man in action.

Rich dipped in the cut as he saw the unknown attacker looking around to see if anyone had witnessed what had just taken place, but from where Rich stood he went unnoticed. As the man turned in the direction of Rich's view, Rich knew who the perp was and what he had just witnessed had become clear. It had been the talk of the town how some young, fine hot redbone had been playing Joe for the past six months, but Rich had no idea the redbone everybody referred to had been Teresa. Rich knew that in the streets all a person had was his or her reputation, so he understood Joe's motives, but it didn't justify them and he knew he couldn't just stand back and watch as Joe did what he knew he intended to do. He waited for Joe to carry Teresa's limp body into the apartment building before he decided to make his move.

He crossed the street with rapid speed, with no time to spare because he knew even though he had a rep on the streets for being a player, Joe had another reputation when it came to women. Rich entered the building with his two .38s in his hands. Rich had no clue as to what apartment Joe had carried Teresa into when he entered the building, and began walking through the hall in hopes of finding some type of indication where they were. Had it not been for his paying close attention, he would have missed the scream.

"S-s-shit," Teresa cursed as she regained consciousness. Upon opening her eyes, the first thing she saw was Player Joe kneeling over her wearing nothing but his boxer shorts. She was sprawled out on the living-room floor in the nude. She was still somewhat dizzy and discombobulated from the blow she had taken to the head, so the reality of the situation had not yet really set in. But whatever the case, Teresa's panic button in the pit of her stomach told her something was not right.

"Joe what the fu—!"

That was all she was able to get out of her mouth before Joe hauled off and back-handed her. "Umph." The blow he delivered split her lip, drawing blood.

"Shut the fuck up. You know what it is, you young cunt. You think you just gonna play me the fuck out like that and get away with it? Bitch, is you crazy?" he barked.

"How you gonna play a player, youngin'?" The slap dazed Teresa, who was stunned by the blow. She tried to recover from the hit and maneuver to get Joe off top of her, but most of her strength had been drained from the blow to her head she had taken earlier. Still, there was no way she was just going to lay there and let this fake player deprive her of the most sacred and precious thing she knew she possessed.

"Muthafucka, get off me," she screamed as she twisted, kicked, and turned, but Joe paid her no mind. He was determined to teach her a lesson.

"Bitch, if you scream or move like that one more time I'm gonna put a bullet right in your pretty-ass face. Now stay still while I handle my business and get what I paid for since your gamin' ass ain't tryin to give it up," Joe said, grabbing the gun from the floor and pointing the barrel directly at Teresa's face. With the other hand, he pulled his manhood out of the slit of his dollar sign–printed boxers.

If looks could kill Joe would have been in his casket waiting to be buried. Teresa ice-grilled him, bringing chills to Joe. It was if her eyes had turned to coal right before him. For a split second, a sense of regret swept over him. He did his best to conceal his inner feeling, replacing it with lust. Teresa knew she was indeed in a no-win situation. She had dealt with more than enough men to know when somebody was serious and the look in Joe's eyes said it all. This was not how Teresa wanted to lose her virginity, but she had no other choice. It was either let Joe have his way with her, and after it was all said and done, she could seek revenge later, or risk taking a shot to the face and really being scarred for life. Either way the odds were against her, and she had no one to blame but herself. She couldn't help but think about how her mother tried to warn her and she had disregarded her words. Now she was being forced against her will to give herself to someone she had no connection with or feelings for.

She squeezed her eyes tightly shut. They became moist with tears as she felt Joe parting her legs. She could feel his hand between her thighs, touching her where no man had ever touched her before. She felt dirty and violated just from the thought of what she knew was to follow.

Joe's mouth watered as he felt the heat generating between her young thighs. Already he had thought about how he would go around town bragging about how he had busted "little dick-teasing" Teresa's cherry. His member throbbed at the thought of Teresa's innocence as he pre-ejaculated from the excitement. He had never been with a virgin before and Teresa's tightness turned him on. He couldn't believe how difficult it was for his middle finger to explore the inside of her. She had made him wait long enough. It was time to take what he had been paying for the past six months. In his mind he began to rationalize and justify what he was about to do, figuring he had technically earned it and it was his to do as he pleased.

Just as he was about to exchange his hand with his manhood to penetrate Teresa, he was interrupted by a loud noise.

As Rich pressed his ear up against the door, he heard Joe's threats. He checked to see whether Joe had been stupid and careless enough to have left the door unlocked, but he hadn't. Rich knew Joe was about to make his move, and he could not let it go down like that, so without hesitation he stepped back and kicked in the apartment door.

"What the hell?" yelled Joe, turning toward the door area. In the blink of an eye Rich was up on Joe with both trey-eights pointed at him.

"Rich?" questioned Joe. "What the fuck you doin' here, man?"

Rich clonked Joe across the head with one of his guns the same way he had seen him do Teresa, knocking him from Teresa's naked body.

"Shut your bitch ass up," commanded Rich as he backed up and closed the apartment door, not once taking his eyes or his guns off Joe.

Hearing a new voice inside the room, Teresa opened her eyes. When she did, she saw Joe lying on the floor next to her, holding his head. Her gaze landed directly on Rich. She wondered who this stranger was who had just come to her rescue and why. Whoever he was, she was grateful and thankful for his good timing and existence. When she noticed his eyes locked on her, a sense of vulnerability overcame her, and it dawned on her that she sat on the floor still in the nude. Conscious of the condition she was in, she balled up into a fetal position.

For a brief moment Rich gazed at Teresa's feminine frame. The first thought that came to mind was *flawless*. In that quick, but deep, stare, he could see her body was intact. Despite the fact, he knew he had to remain focused. To stand there and entertain such thoughts would make him no better than Player Joe. The only difference would be he only thought it, Joe acted on it.

He knew that the last thing Teresa needed was to feeling more uncomfortable than she already did, especially in her condition. Rich attempted to console her.

"You a'ight?" he asked. She nodded while wiping her stained face.

Looking around, Teresa didn't see her clothes anywhere. Rich looked around himself without locating them. Sensing her discomfort, he unbuttoned his blue silk shirt and gave it to her, the whole time never taking his eyes off of Joe. "Put this on."

"Man, who the fuck is you? Super-Save-a-Ho?" exclaimed Joe.

He was just now regaining his senses, after being caught off guard by Rich. It was apparent, thought Joe, that Rich either did not know who he was or was just plain high. But Joe knew who he was, and before the day ended, it was Joe's intent to introducing himself to Rich properly. He made a mental note to teach Rich two lessons. One, who he was and two, to mind his own business.

Joe's thoughts were quickly interrupted. Rich walked over to him and grabbed him by the face, sticking the barrel of one of his .38s into his mouth. "Didn't I tell you to shut the fuck up, you pussy-takin' muthafucka?" Rich spat. "Yeah, I know your MO, chump."

Joe widened his eyes. He knew it was not in his best interest to utter another word. Aside from the gun now shoved in his mouth, Joe could see in Rich's face he meant business. He had seen the same hardened look on other killers' faces to know Rich had killed before and wouldn't hesitate to kill again.

Rich turned around and took a quick glance back to make sure Teresa had put the shirt on he had given her, but when he looked she was nowhere to be found. He assumed she had gone to get properly dressed. As he stood over Joe with his gun in his mouth, he wondered what he was going to do from there. Initially when he decided to rescue Teresa, that was as far as his plan had gone, and he had accomplished what he had set out to do. He was now at a stuck point. Any other time he would have just slumped Joe because he had killed jokers for less, but it had always been for a reason, whether business or personal, and this particular incident was neither of the two since he had no arrangements or connection with Teresa. He had acted strictly on impulse, and now he was faced with a dilemma.

Though Joe was not known for being a killer, it was known he had killed before. Rich knew if he were to let Joe go, there was a strong possibility he might want to seek revenge. That was simply the code of the streets. On the other hand, if he bodied Joe, he would have to worry about witnesses—or in this case, *a* witness. Regardless of the fact that Rich had just saved her from a situation that would have most likely scarred her for life, when it was all said and done and the heat came down, Teresa could tie him to the murder. At that moment, the thought of killing both Joe and Teresa crossed his mind. He instantly shook off the notion. It would defeat his whole purpose for involving himself in the situation, he reasoned. The only logical plan he could come up with was to let Joe live momentarily and catch him another day before he had the opportunity to catch him first.

"Stand the fuck up!" ordered Rich. Joe hesitated before making any type of move. He knew how Rich played out in the streets, so he wasn't trying to take any chances since Rich could have been trying to fake him out. "I know you heard what I said. Get your punk ass up." Rich snatched Joe up by the arm.

"A'ight man, damn!" Joe shot back, snatching away from Rich.

Rich hit Joe again, and Joe screamed.

"Next time it ain't gonna be the back of my gun that I hit you with," stated Rich.

To show his patience was wearing thin and he was growing tired of Joe's cockiness, Rich contemplated shooting Joe in his kneecaps, but reserved the thought. He knew that he'd see Joe again. It was destined. And when he did, there would be no talking—not verbally anyway—only with bullets.

"Put your muthafuckin' clothes back on and get the fuck up outta here 'fore I leave you here not breathin'," Rich threatened. Without hesitation Joe began reaching for his pants, making sure not to take his eyes off Rich. When he bent down his semi-erection slid through the slit of his boxers, causing Rich to turn his back to Joe.

"This joker," Rich said under his breath. "Hurry the fuck up and put ya shit on 'fore I change my mind."

That was all the lead Joe needed. He saw an opportunity and intended to take full advantage of it. Rich was just about to turn back around after giving Joe time to get dressed, when he saw Teresa appear before him with an all-black .25 automatic pointed his way. He couldn't believe what he was witnessing. *What part of the game was this?* he thought. Had Joe actually been Teresa's pimp? At this point, Rich regretted changing his mind, thinking he should have gone with his first instinct and bodied both Joe and Teresa. Rich could see in her eyes that Teresa was in kill mode. There was no time to think. Rich's only hope was to get a shot off first before Teresa did and make it count. Before Rich was able to react or raise his own weapon the shots rang out.

Unfazed by the four shots, Rich raised his twin revolvers with murder on his mind. Had it not been for the loud *thud* behind him, Teresa would have been riddled with shots and pinned against the wall from the impact of Rich's cannons. Teresa's heart pulsated through her blouse. She too knew how close she had just come to meeting her maker. Rich turned to see Joe's lifeless body sprawled out on the wooden floor with the gun still in his hand.

Joe had retrieved his .32 that had fallen when Rich had first burst in and knocked him to the floor. His adrenaline began working overtime at the thought of killing Rich. He was positive after today his street credibility would be at an all-time high for killing someone with as much status as the man he was about to get the drop on. After all, this was Richie Gunz he was about to kill. He had no problem with taking the credit, despite trying to kill Rich in a cowardly fashion by shooting him in the back. To him, when it came to the rules of the game, he was never known for playing fair.

Once he took care of Rich and got him out the way, Joe had every intention on picking up where he had left off with Teresa. He began raising his pistol with ease, hoping that Rich didn't turn back around so soon. As he raised his gun half level, Joe saw Teresa appear. She was holding something in her hands, but he couldn't make out what it was. It wasn't until the four shots ripped through his chest, piercing his heart, that Joe realized that what she had possessed in her hands was a gun. By then, it was too late. He was already slipping away. Instantly he fell to the floor with his .32 revolver still in hand.

Rich turned around and saw that the noise he had heard was Joe's lifeless body hitting the floor.

Teresa stood there, still in shock at what she had done, but she couldn't allow Joe to kill the man who had come to her aid moments ago. She owed him, and his first payment had been Joe's last breath.

Rich walked over to Joe's body, spotting the .32 in his hands, and imagined how close he had come to being the one sprawled out on the floor instead of Joe. Thanks to Teresa, his life had been spared. He thought about how close he had come to killing her and felt bad for entertaining it. He had been worried about her being able to implicate him if he had killed Joe, but now he was the one who could tie her to the murder. How quickly the tables turned, Rich thought.

He knew it was just a matter of time before the cops would be crawling all over the place. Rich was sure someone had heard the gunshots and called them. He knew he had to make some quick decisions. "Sweetheart, we gotta blow this joint," he said as Teresa stood there in a trance, trying to make out Rich's words.

"You hear me? We gotta get outta here."

Snapping out of it, Teresa acknowledged him. "Yeah, we do."

"A'ight then, go snatch up what you can take with you, things that are important. You can't stay here no more and you sure as hell can't never come back."

Teresa knew that to be true because if she ever got caught there she would surely be thrown in jail. Although she felt she could handle being locked up, she was not trying to see there any time soon. She ran into her bedroom to gather her personal and important belongings while Rich waited. When she returned holding two big suitcases, Rich grabbed one and they exited together, never looking back.

"Get this little muthafucka up outta me," screamed Teresa.

The four years she had been with Rich had turned her into one of the most ruthless females from the Chesapeake area. Though her beauty was misconstrued as feminine, her demeanor was a contradiction to her physical appearance. She was so tough she refused the anesthesia that would help with the labor pain of the pregnancy the doctor suggested, and voted against a

C-section in spite of the difficulties of the natural birth she was experiencing. After what seemed like millions of hours in labor, a breakthrough had come about.

"Okay! Okay! The baby is coming," the doctor yelled with relief. Teresa began to push harder as she felt something busting through her inner thighs. It felt as if she was being split in half and the pain was excruciating, but like the trouper she was, she endured the process.

"Just a little more," the doctor said. Rich stood by watching from over the doctor's shoulder. The average man would have turned away, some even would have gotten sick, but not Rich. All the blood he had seen in his life, from all the lives he had taken, had prepared him for this night. All the blood between Teresa's legs could not compare to the lifetime of blood he had spilled. Rich saw the little figure appear and wondered what it was. He couldn't tell due to the umbilical cord, but the doctor's reaction confirmed his thoughts.

"It's a boy," he said as he cut the cord.

The doctor turned the baby over on his stomach and smacked him on the behind and that's when all hell broke loose.

The next sound was the doctor hitting the delivery room's floor. Rich knocked the doctor clean out, with his son still in the doctor's hands. All the other nurses and doctors were astonished at Rich's behavior, as they all took steps back, not wanting any problems. Rich stood over the doctor and picked his son up, and the baby cried. "Muthafucka, you bet not ever put your hands on my son again. Ain't nobody on this planet gonna ever put their hands on my kid as long as he live," shouted Rich, hovering over the doctor, who lay sprawled out on the floor. "You dig?"

Everybody was so afraid they all agreed. They were so focused on Rich that no one had paid any attention to the amount of blood Teresa had been losing. By the time the police arrived and took Rich away, Teresa had hemorrhaged and bled to death and little John Doe was all alone.

Chapter Two

Rich was arrested on assault charges at the hospital the day his son was born. He was told by the arresting officer that the mother of his child did not survive. Teresa died right on the delivery table. As Rich sat in the bullpen of the Norfolk city jail he wept for the loss of Teresa, the woman he had grown attached to over the past five years. It was the first time in his life he had ever cried, externally anyway, and it was a feeling he wasn't particularly fond of. He wiped his face in an attempt to regain his composure. He thought of his newborn son and how without notice he had been forced to raise him on his own, motherless. He had been on his own for quite some time and had practically raised himself, but to raise another human being—a young infant at that—was an entirely different ball game and was his biggest challenge as a man.

March 9 was the day that changed Rich's life forever, one he would never forget. He sat impatiently waiting for the bails bondsman to post his bond, anxious to go back to the hospital and claim his son.

When Rich arrived, some of the nurses remembered his sudden outburst and the loss of his child's mother and had mixed feelings seeing him again. Some blamed his ignorance for her death while others felt compassionate and sympathy for his loss. One young white nurse had the heart and the courtesy enough to escort Rich to the window where little John Doe lay. When they reached the maternity ward, Rich recognized his son instantly without the nurse having to point him out. It was as though he himself had spit him out. Rich saw the strong resemblance of him in his son. The only thing Rich could see he possessed of Teresa so far was his smooth, baby golden-brown–toned complexion. If Rich didn't know any better he would have sworn Teresa had been creeping on him with another man. He himself was charcoal black; Teresa, light bronze.

He was prideful as he stood at the glass.

"Sir," the nurse called out to him, breaking his fixated stare at his son.

"Yeah, what's up?"

"Uh, well, you know your child doesn't have a name yet," the nurse said nervously.

It hadn't dawned on him that Teresa hadn't named their kid before she'd passed away. They had discussed it many times throughout her pregnancy. If it was a girl they would name her Mercedes, that way the they would always have one, but if it was a boy, Rich insisted he had a name that stood out, a name that he would be able to represent, that would show a great deal of strength.

"How do I go about naming my kid?" he asked the nurse, putting her at ease.

"Right this way, I'll show you," she replied, shooting Rich a smile. He followed the nurse as her young hips swayed in her pink-and-white nurse's outfit.

Had it been under different circumstances and a different time, Rich might have gotten at the white girl because it was obvious she was attracted to him. She flirtatiously threw her hips, which were wide for a white woman, hoping he was watching from behind. He was too. The truth be told, she was actually turned on by Rich's performance in the room earlier that day. Coming from a middle- class family, she had been attracted to and had dealings with so- called "bad boys" since her rebellious days as a teenager, not to mention the fact she liked men the way she liked her coffee, dark and strong, and Rich fit the profile.

As they walked steps away from each other they came up on a desk. The girl went behind the desk, only to return with the form Rich needed to fill out stating his was little John Doe's birth father. She told him she'd return momentarily, giving him both time and space to fill out the form. Rich glanced over it, then began filling it out as best he could. In all the years he had known Teresa, all he knew about her personal information was her full name and birth date, which was all he was able to provide on the application. Teresa Laton Freeman, birth date July 2, 1958 was what he filled out. He then filled in his full birth name and date of birth: Richard Anthony Robinson Jr., March 3, 1956. When he reached the column that required his son's name, he began writing it out. Rich named his son Treacherous Antwan Freeman. Initially his son was supposed to have borne his last name, but in memory of his mother, Rich gave him her last name. Antwan was Rich's grandfather's name, and the name Treacherous spoke for itself. Rich was determined to give his son a name he would have to live up to. Although he was only a day old, when he grew up Rich was determined to make sure his son knew his father was a gangster, the same thing he would raise him to become someday.

The white nurse returned just as Rich was finishing up the form. She took it, assured him it was filled out properly, then told him his son would be able to go home in two more days after they had finished running tests to make sure he was healthy and there were no complications. She slipped him her number and told him to call her and she would keep him updated on his son's status.

Two days passed and Rich arrived back at the hospital to pick up little Treacherous. Against his better judgment, he had been sexing the white nurse, who he found to be a super-freak, for the past two days. Rich walked down the corridor to where he was told he'd be able to pick his son up. It did not surprise him to see the young white girl standing there as if she had been waiting for him when he reached the maternity ward. He had already anticipated as much.

"Hey love," she addressed him, twirling her finger through one of her golden locks. The thought of what Rich had been doing to her body for the past two days had her floating. When she woke up, she was disappointed to find that he was already gone, but she knew she would see him at the hospital today.

"Wassup," Rich replied drily.

"I missed you this morning." Her giddiness rubbed Rich the wrong way. He knew it was time to put an end to the charade.

"Dig, find you a toy to play with 'cause I'm not the one. It was cool, but that's all it was, no more, no less," Rich stated before turning his back on her and walking toward the receptionist's desk. The white girl was crushed by his treatment. The elderly white woman at the desk had overheard some of what Rich had said to her colleague. She had been inconspicuously observing the encounter between the two. It was evident to the elderly nurse that something was going on between Rich and the young white nurse and she did not agree with the way he had just treated the girl. She shot Rich a dirty look as he approached.

"What the fuck is your problem lady?" he questioned, already knowing the reason for the look.

The elderly nurse was instantly filled with fear. She had no idea she was so obvious. She was at a loss for words and tempted to call security but thought better of it. She had heard about the episode in the delivery room and didn't want to upset Rich anymore then she already had.

"Th—there's no problem sir, how may I help you," she uttered, trying to make light of the situation.

Rich couldn't help but laugh to himself. It never failed with white people, he thought. When you're nice to them they were nasty to you, but the moment you got nasty back, they were the nicest people in the world.

"I'm here to pick up my son, Treacherous Freeman."

"Yes, just a moment." The elderly nurse fumbled nervously to assist him. "You can have seat. Someone will be with you in a moment, sir."

Her words fell on deaf ears. Rich remained standing at the desk, waiting for his son. Everyone was all too glad to see Rich leave, at least everyone but the young white nurse. She watched from afar with tear-filled eyes as he signed his son out of the hospital. He had everyone on edge, including security. They had all seen the aftermath of the doctor's face from the one blow Rich had hit him with, and wanted no part of the man. Security was thankful that Rich had complied without any incident or resistance that day. To them, he had the look of someone who could do some serious damage if he had to.

Rich put the hooded snowsuit on his newborn to protect him from the winter hawk that awaited them on the outside of the hospital. Although it was March, spring had not yet come. He grabbed his son with one arm, attempting to leave the hospital with the intention of never returning. He vowed that baby Treacherous would be his first and only child, just as his son's mother was his first and only love.

Chapter Three

The first three and a half years of raising his son was a learning experience for Rich between warming bottles, changing diapers, and adjusting to Treacherous's sleeping schedule. The one thing he was grateful for was the fact that his son was not a crier. Not since they had left the hospital and he was arrested for knocking the doctor out for putting his hands on Treacherous, had he heard his son cry. He wondered whether there was something wrong, but excused it when Treacherous spoke his first word, which was *Dad*, often coming out sounding like *bad*. Rich would often reply, "That's right, son, you bad."

Treacherous's childhood was a little more peculiar than most growing up. Rich never brought him any toys like the other kids in his Portsmouth neighborhood. Rich was raised to believe toys made you soft, and he wasn't about to raise a punk. Instead, he substituted Treacherous's toys with his own real guns, which he had plenty of. By the time Treacherous was six years old he could name every caliber of handgun and a few semiautomatics and by the age of eight he knew how to take them apart, clean, and oil them up. In Rich's mind, there was nothing wrong with the way he was raising his son. Rich never really let Treacherous hang outside in the Tidewater Park projects where they lived, because he didn't want Treacherous making friends out there. He told Treacherous when he was questioned that it was not good to have a lot of friends because you never know when you might have to do something to them; if there were no attachments then there would be no remorse or regret later. At the time Treacherous didn't really understand his father's words, but he both trusted and respected his dad, so he figured whatever the reason meant it was for his own good.

Not only had Treacherous grown up knowing about guns, he was also trained, skilled, and educated in sports, boxing in particular. Rich was known to be nice with his hands in boxing as well as street fighting, so he taught Treacherous all he knew. He made him practice every night before he took a bath and went to sleep, often waking up in the morning too sore to climb out of bed to go to school from throwing so many one-handed jabs on each arm and combinations. Treacherous had no way of the knowing the significance behind his upbringing. Although he only went outside when Rich took him, Treacherous knew he lived in a rough neighborhood, but he wasn't afraid. There was no need to be. He was Richie Gunz's kid.

Everywhere he went, Rich took Treacherous with him. Treacherous could remember the first time he had actually saw his dad do what he called work. He and his father sat in the little rusted Chevy, just waiting. Treacherous had no idea what they were waiting for. When a tall, dapper man exited the store they were parked in front of, Treacherous noticed his father's eyes grow cold.

"Wait here," Rich told him as he made his way out of the car.

Treacherous watched as his father, dressed in all black, approached the tall man. Treacherous heard the confrontation going on outside of the car as he witnessed the scene with his own eyes.

"You thought it was a game," Treacherous heard his father shout as he forcefully grabbed the tall man around the neck with his free hand.

"*Pleeeaassse* man, I gotta—"

Treacherous jumped each time the shots rang out. The four slugs tore into the dapper man as he bellied over and dropped to the ground in the middle of the street. Treacherous watched as Rich leaned over and stuck his hand into the slain man's pockets. He retrieved the wad of cash from the front pocket, shoved it into his own pocket, and calmly made his way back to the car. Treacherous was wide- eyed as Rich got in and drove off without uttering a word. And neither did Treacherous. It was then that Treacherous knew what type of man his father was.

For his thirteenth birthday, Rich took his son to the local strip bar, where Treacherous was well underage, but because he was Richie Gunz's kid, nothing was said. Treacherous couldn't believe his eyes. There were half-naked, topless women scattered all over the establishment in all shapes, sizes, and colors. Some were pretty while others were not, Treacherous thought. He recognized a few of the women who frequented where he and his father lived.

One particular night his attention was drawn to the loud noises he heard coming from his father's bedroom. Not knowing what to make of it, Treacherous peered into his dad's room through the keyhole, only to see that Rich was naked and positioned behind one of the strippers, pulling her hair and ramming his body into hers as she faced the door. Judging by her expressions, one would have thought the young stripper was in pain, but Treacherous knew better. Rich had already schooled him about sex, and though he had never experienced it personally, Treacherous knew the cries were not painful ones. He knew the girl would not have been telling his father to give it to her harder if she was not enjoying herself.

***

Treacherous had only seen one picture of his mother in his life, an old one that his father kept in his wallet, but as he looked around, he could see no one in the club whose beauty could compare to hers, not even one of the numerous women his dad brought home. His mother was the most beautiful woman he had ever seen in his thirteen years of living. Every year, since his birth, Rich and Treacherous visited Teresa's grave on Treacherous's birthday.

Rich guided Treacherous to the bar. He ordered two double shots of Hennessy cognac and two Guinness beers. Treacherous thought that to be a lot of alcohol for his father. Only when Rich slid one of the double shots and beer over in his direction did Treacherous discover one order was for him.

"Drink that, it'll put hair on your chest," Rich said with his signature grin as the bartender matched Rich's smile.

Treacherous hesitated before grabbing the glass as all eyes were on him. He no longer felt like a young boy in an adult setting, but rather a young man. Treacherous had never drunk before in his life, but knew he had to drink what sat in front of him. If he refused, his father would be disappointed, and that was the last thing he wanted to do. He grabbed the glass and put it up to his face. The aroma of the cognac had a strong but smooth smell to it. He parted his lips and began to drink as the onlookers watched him in amazement.

Treacherous's eyes instantly began to water. The Hennessy scorched his throat as it went down, setting his insides on fire. Knowing what was taking place, Rich told him to chase it with the Guinness. Treacherous grabbed the cold beer. The Guinness was bitter but did the job, soothing the flames in his throat and the pit of his stomach. It was as though he had just drank a glass of rocks mixed with dirt. Rich smiled again at his son.

He knew what he was thinking because Guinness was an acquired taste. As Treacherous put the beer down he noticed Rich motioning to one of the exotic dancers to come to where he sat. She had been dancing on the pole behind the bar the whole time they had been up there. She was about five feet seven, petite, brown-skinned with large breasts for her little frame, and she was fairly cute. As she stepped down from the stage, Treacherous sat there staring at her, mesmerized. The closer she came, the wider Treacherous's eyes became. It was as if her body was like a 3-D movie to Treacherous, only this was real life, he knew. Treacherous didn't realize the drinks had instantly taken effect on him. By now the girl stood behind the bar in front of Rich and Treacherous with her breasts revealing their bareness. Treacherous's thirteen-year-old young manhood began to stiffen at the sight.

"Hey, Rich," she shouted over the music

"What's up, Diamond?"

"Who's the little man you got with you, with his fine self?" she asked.

"My son," Rich announced proudly.

"Your son?" She seemed surprised. As many times as she had gone to Rich's place, she never knew he had a child. Though their relationship was strictly sexual and business, she couldn't believe she had never seen or heard anything indicating Rich had a kid.

"Yeah, my son. Today is his birthday, and I want you to give him a lap dance," Rich said all in one breath.

Diamond smiled, causing Treacherous to smile, although he had no idea what a lap dance was.

"Okay," Diamond replied without hesitation. The bar had been slow all day and she could really use the money, she thought. Especially since Rich was such a good tipper.

"How old is he?" she asked

"Thirteen."

Diamond frowned. She thought Treacherous was a little older. She played him for fifteen at the least, which was the youngest she had ever performed for.

"You sure you want me to give him a lap dance?"

"What I ask you for?" Rich snapped.

"Okay, Rich. Dag, you aint gotta get all like that, I'll do it."

"That's my girl," Rich calmly stated. "Charlie, get Diamond whatever she's drinkin'."

"You got it, Gunz," the bartender retorted. "What'cha having, beautiful?" he then directed to Diamond.

"Lemme get a double tequila."

Diamond held her drink up to Rich and threw it back. The bitter taste of the tequila burned slow as it traveled down her throat. That was her fourth double of the night, but she had become immune to the strong drink. It was only when she came to the bar club that she drank hard-core liquor to take the edge off. Just as the drink, Diamond had become fully immune to her profession.

Treacherous didn't know what was going on. He was too busy enjoying the feeling of the intoxicants, caught up in the rapture of Al Green's lyrics, which filled the hole-in-the-wall juke joint. Rich laughed as he got his son's attention.

"Come on, let's go over here," he said, pointing to the table in the corner. When Treacherous got up off the stool he slightly stumbled and staggered as he followed behind his father.

"Easy, champ," said Rich as he helped his son catch his balance. They both walked to the table, and Diamond came shortly after. This time she stood right in front of Treach and he looked up at her.

"Happy Birthday, little man," she said as she straddled him. Treacherous didn't know what to do. He had no clue as to why this woman had just climbed on top of him. When he looked at his father, Rich only gave him an approving smile. That assured Treacherous that all was well. After all, his dad never steered him wrong. Diamond began to slow grind her hips and pelvis into Treacherous. His erection grew under her, and she began focusing on that specific spot as she buried his face into her voluptuous breasts. She was only eighteen, a baby herself, so her body was still intact. Treacherous took in the scent of the girl's cheap perfume combined with perspiration. He could not breathe. Rich sipped on his drink as Treacherous received his lap dance from Diamond.

Diamond worked her body with skill to the rhythm of the music that filled the air. Diamond decided to give Treacherous a lap dance that he would never forget. She wanted to add a little something extra to her routine. With Treacherous turning the age of thirteen she felt that this should be a memorable moment for him. Diamond reflected back to the time when she herself was turning thirteen, still young and innocent, until she was deprived of that innocence by one of her mother's lovers. Diamond shook off the thought as she rode Treacherous with one hand around his neck, while she unbuttoned his pants with the other. Treacherous was too caught up in the mood to even notice. Between the alcohol and the fact that he had a grown woman on top of him, he was in heaven at that moment.

It wasn't until he felt something warm on his young manhood that he became alarmed. Diamond slid her hand inside of Treacherous's pants and found his penis. She was surprised to discover that it was not as small as she had thought it to be, but then again, being who his father was, she should have figured as much. She began to massage his not-yet manhood, and felt the pre-cum on the tip of his head.

Treacherous was moaning and squirming from the feeling that Diamond's hand was causing him. He had never felt this way before in his life. He wasn't aware that it even existed. After getting him nice and erect, Diamond leaned in and kissed Treacherous on the lips, forcing her tongue in his mouth, parting his lips. This was Treacherous's first kiss. He had no idea what he was doing. Diamond's tongue tasted a combination of sweet and salty, thought Treacherous, as he tried to follow her lead and return her kiss, but was thrown off by the heat and wetness on his penis. His male member felt like it had whenever he sat in a tub of hot bathwater, but better.

Diamond slid her G-string to the side and straddled Treacherous's penis, taking him inside of her. Rich was watching what was taking place and said nothing. He knew that it was time for his son to become a man and he wanted to be there when it happened. By now Treacherous realized what was taking place and tried to relax, but he couldn't. The motion of Diamond's hips was so powerful that he tried to meet her thrust for thrust just so she wouldn't drown him in her small ocean.

"You like this, sugah?" Diamond purred as she gyrated her hips into Treacherous.

"Uh- huh," Treacherous answered as he continued to keep up with Diamond's pace.

Diamond couldn't believe that she was actually getting pleasure from a thirteen-year-old. Each time she grinded a certain way Treacherous would be there to meet her with his penis brushing up against her clit occasionally, sending her into orbit. She climaxed twice while riding him.

She was actually enjoying the ordeal but now it was time to end. Diamond wrapped her arms around Treacherous's neck and began to ride him like a wild stallion, causing him to lose control. This was her specialty. She had put the same move on many men on many of nights when she was trying to make a fast dollar. Treacherous wasn't ready for this part of the game. He layed back, powerless, while Diamond did what she did best. As he sat there, a funny feeling came over Treacherous. He began to tense up and jerk as his left leg cramped up. He grabbed Diamond's waist, trying to get her to cease because he thought she was hurting him. Diamond thought she was hurting him and began to slow her pace, but then realized what was going on and stopped. Mission accomplished. Treacherous buried his face in her chest and held her as his clear fluids poured into her. When she thought he was done, she got up slowly.

"Happy Birthday, little man," she said, kissing Treacherous on the cheek. "And thank you." Treacherous had no idea why, but Rich knew. He saw in Diamond's face that she had reached an orgasm, if not more. Rich gave Diamond a hundred dollars and took his son home for the night.

Chapter Four

"Mr. Robinson I'm sorry to have called you in today. I'm sure you are a very busy man, but here at MAAP Elementary we take these matters very seriously and fighting will not be tolerated at our school," the principal expressed to Rich.

Rich really had no patience with the white woman, nor did he want to be sitting there listening to her reprimand him about his son as though he was a mere schoolkid. His first instinct was to pull out one of the two guns he had on him and shove it in the principal's mouth to get her to shut up, but he knew that wouldn't be the appropriate thing to do, not while he was trying to be a respectable parent in front of his son, so he set his street mentality aside and tried to use a much more effective approach when dealing with the woman, not aggressive but assertive.

"Listen, Ms. Chambers, I understand what you are saying and I agree, but my kid is not no bad kid and he don't just go around jumping on other people's kids, so before you start talking about what you will and won't tolerate in your school, you need to get all the facts to a situation instead of just blaming my boy, making him out to be some type of bully or something. My son is a humble boy and he is will behaved. He has home training and he has discipline, so tell me, Ms. Chambers, what was the reason for my son and the other boy fighting in the first place, and why are only me and my son the only ones in your office and the other child and his parents aren't?"

The white principal's face became red as Rich talked. She had never been talked to like that in her life by any other parent in her whole seventeen years as a principal, and she resented the fact that this man sat before her questioning her as if she were on trial. She had never dealt with such a disgruntled parent as Rich. She was determined not to back down. It was apparent to her where Treacherous got his temper from.

"Mr. Robinson, first of all, why two kids were fighting is not the issue here, because in case you aren't aware, children fight over some meaningless things. But if you want to know," she continued in a dry tone, "it's been confirmed by several other students that your son threw the first punch and the other boy never hit back. For your information, the other child and his parents are in the school's infirmary because your son caused the other student's nose to bleed. He also has a black-and-blue right eye, and he knocked one of the boy's front teeth out. Now I don't know what type of guerilla-warfare tactics you have been teaching him at home, but like I said before, that will not be tolerated in this school and this is no place for such behavior. Now, I don't know whether the little boy's parents will pursue this and press charges, but I suggest you be prepared. You say that your son—"

Rich quickly interrupted her. "You don't know nothing about my son, lady. Yeah, kids do fight for dumb shit, but not my kid. He knows better, but if he did, then I'm going to deal with him. It may not mean nothing to you, but it does to me."

Treacherous sat there listening the whole time as his father verbally reprimanded his principal.

"Treach."

"Huh?"

"You know I don't tolerate lying, right?"

"I know, Dad," Treacherous replied, looking his father straight in the eyes.

"So what happened?"

"I was outside on the yard at lunchtime just hanging by myself when these three boys stepped to me and started talking mess to me."

"Like what?"

"They started saying that I'm retarded, that's why I ain't got no friends and stuff like that."

"And what did you say?"

"I just said I ain't retarded and I don't need no friends."

"Then what?"

"Then one of the boys got all up in my face and said I was a punk, and I said I ain't no punk, you a punk, then he said your mother a punk, B-I-T-C-H," Treacherous spelled out, knowing better than to use the word. "And that's when I hit him."

After hearing the story, Rich felt his son's actions were justifiable and he supported him 100 percent. Rich redirected his attention to the principal.

"Maybe not in your book, but in mine, my son did what he was supposed to do, Ms. Chambers, whether you or the board of education or whoever like it or not. I don't know if you are aware, but my son's mother is deceased. She passed away while giving birth to Treacherous. Now, I don't know where you come from, but where we come from if you talk about or disrespect someone's mother then you in violation and subjected to anything. Whether you tell me that you agree or not I know you do, especially being a woman, and seeing as though you have two sons of your own in that picture right there. Can you imagine how my son felt hearing that?"

Ms. Chambers would never admit to it, but she now understood Treacherous's violent attack on the student, but instead of condoning Rich's son's actions, she tried to deal with the situation according to her position. "I understand you being upset, and hearing this makes a world of difference. Treacherous, if you just tell me the other two boys' names I will deal with them appropriately because they had no right talking about you like that."

"Whoa! Whoa," interjected Rich. "My son ain't no snitch. He told me why he fought because his father asked him, but he ain't here to get nobody in trouble. What's done is done, that's it. Whatever you do from here on out that's on you, but you ain't getting no help on this end, lady."

"Mr. Robinson, what type of examples are you setting for your son? What are you raising him to become? He's a child, not a—"

Again Rich cut her off, reaching his breaking point.

"Bitch, who you think you talking to like that? I let you talk slick since I been in your funky-ass office, but all that shit is dead. You can't tell me shit about me and mine. However I choose to raise my son is my muthafuckin' business. Everybody don't live in a big house with a white picket muthafuckin' fence happily ever after. I come from the real world. Don't try to sit here with all that righteous bullshit. You don't know me, and you can't judge me. Only God can do that. Matter of fact, I'm taking my son up out this soft brainwashing-ass school. Get me my son's records right now before I tear this muthafucka up," he demanded. By now the principal had practically wet her pants out of fear of Rich's behavior.

She didn't respond. Instead, the principal went to the file cabinet, pulled Treacherous's school records out, and gave them to Rich, who then got up. Treacherous followed his father, neither of the two looking back. Treacherous was honored to have a father like Rich, who had his back no matter what.

As they walked out of the principal's office together, as soon as the door closed Ms. Chambers sat in her chair with her beet-red face in her hands and began to cry. She had never been so afraid in her life. She didn't come from that type of background and couldn't understand why Treacherous's father was so hostile. She was tempted to call the authorities but thought better of it. Ms. Chambers did not want to risk Rich coming back at a later date. As Rich and Treacherous walked through the door, all of the school faculty and students who were outside the office stared at them in silence. They all had heard how Rich had spoken to their principal, setting her straight the way they wished they had the heart to do. Some of the adults nodded to Rich, while some of the students said good-bye to Treacherous. By the time they had left the building and exited on Rich's motorcycle, it was all over school how Treacherous's dad regulated principal Chambers and told her how his son did the right thing by beating up the duke of the school. Treacherous hadn't been aware of the kid being the duke until Rich transferred him to the roughest school in Portsmouth: Churchland Elementary. What he didn't know was that Treacherous's reputation followed him from MAAP. The whole school had already formulated an opinion about him. Some of them feared him, while all respected him. They knew the reputation of the other kid and knew that if Treacherous could take someone like him then he was not to be reckoned with.

Chapter Five

Treacherous had just graduated elementary with the intention of going to Churchland Junior High, but Rich informed him they would be moving out of the projects into a home in Portsmouth and he'd be attending W.E. Water, which was an all-black school and not too far from where they were moving. Although Treacherous still had no friends, he had grown fond of the projects where he had been raised. He had gotten used to walking home from school, seeing the local hustlers out selling their drugs or stomping somebody out around there who tried to leave a dice game with the winnings. At night he would hear gunshots going off because Tidewater Park projects would be beefing with the Diggs Park projects, which was right across from the Tidewater and was just as thorough.

Everybody knew the Tidewater Park and Diggs Park boys were the best fighters, but often a lot of shooting transpired and a lot of bodies popped up. Oak Leaf Park projects was another spot Tidewater beefed with. No one liked going up in there because it was only one way in and one way out of the spot where Treacherous grew up. Tidewater beefed with everybody. The area in which Treacherous had been raised would be viewed as highly dangerous. It had a reputation for being wild, but to someone like Treacherous it was the best. Rich had just started letting Treacherous go outside after his first fight at Churchland Elementary, setting off a spree of fights. Other kids who thought they were tough had heard about

Treacherous's fighting skills and wanted to test them. They found out the hard way just how nice Treacherous was with his hands. By the time Treacherous had turned thirteen his fighting record in the hood was 8-0, and the old and young heads respected his hand game and his gangster all around the board after his last fight. One day when Treacherous was coming home from school he crossed paths with one of the young hustlers who was four years his senior. As Treacherous walked passed the kid he heard his name called out. Treacherous stopped at the sound of his name being called. When he looked he saw the kid standing there, gesturing for him to come to where he stood with some type of bill in his hand. Treacherous recognized the kid, who was known as Bear, huddled up with four other kids he knew to be local drug dealers. He was a bully who picked on the younger kids.

Treacherous was not afraid of Bear, who was twice his size. His father had taught him that it wasn't the size of the person but the size of their heart and the bigger they are the harder they fall, not to mention the fact that he had been taking his twelfth birthday present with him wherever he went. He contemplated on walking over there to see what Bear wanted. Whatever it was, Treacherous knew it wasn't anything good, the way Bear and the other boys smirked, trying to hold their laughter.

Bear motioned for Treacherous again, and this time he went over.

"Oh, I thought you was gonna act like you ain't hear me and keep going like a li'l bitch," Bear joked.

At the sound of that Treacherous instantly regretted coming to see what Bear wanted. "I ain't no bitch," he replied sternly.

"Yo chill, li'l Treach, I'm just fuckin' with you. Here, take this and run to the store for me right quick," Bear ordered, holding out a five-dollar bill. Treacherous looked at him as if he had just spoken Chinese, then spun around and began walking off.

Bear reached out and grabbed him by the shoulder. "Yo, you hear what the—"

That's as far as he got before Treacherous grabbed his hand, stepped to the side, and hip- tossed Bear to the ground. The other four boys stood there, stunned, as Bear lay there flat on his back. Treacherous stood waiting for Bear to get up as the other hustlers and spectators gathered. As bad as they wanted to, none of the boys made a move to jump Treacherous because they knew who they'd have to answer to. Bear had an embarrassed expression on his face as he got up. His ego and pride had been bruised. There was only one way to redeem himself, he thought. He fumbled to reach under his shirt. At that point he used emotion over intellect. Already on point, Treacherous drew his birthday present in the blink of an eye, switched the safety off in rapid speed and skill. The shot came out of nowhere, surprising everyone, including Bear.

Bear screamed in agony. "This li'l mu'fucka shot me."

Bear saw his hand was leaking through his shirt. Before he could get his gun out Treacherous had beat him to the draw. Not sure what to do, Bear's boys stared at Treacherous in awe.

As an extra precaution, Treacherous drew his weapon on Bear's friends.

"Whoa, li'l Treach, you got it, baby," one of the boys said, throwing his hands up in the air as the others followed suit.

Treacherous kneeled and disarmed Bear of the 9 mm he possessed under his shirt, never taking his eyes off of him. Still with gun drawn, Treacherous made his way home. It was from that day forward that Treacherous was no longer looked at as just being Richie Gunz's kid, but as little thorough-ass Treacherous. When Rich found out what took place that day no one saw or heard from Bear since and no one dared to ask.

Chapter Six

W.E. Water Junior High School's reputation spoke for itself. Some of the toughest kids from the streets attended there, and many legends came out of it. This was the only all-black junior high in Portsmouth, so it was just like one big projects to Treacherous. Just like the school he attended, Treacherous's rep spoke for itself as well. He had only been back in school for about three months and had already pounded the duke of the school and began collecting all the punk dues the duke had collected. Kids who paid the old duke insisted Treach take their money. They thought by paying him it would keep the old duke from beating them up and at the same time they figured they could buy Treacherous's friendship.

He took the money because his father told him not to turn down anything but his collar, but he would never protect those who paid him nor would he befriend them. He actually liked the fact that people gave him money just out of fear and on the strength of who he was. In his mind, there wasn't anything wrong with accepting the other kids' money. He actually enjoyed being paid for just being himself. He saved every cent of what was given to him. Treacherous dreamed of buying a motorcycle like his father's when he got older and knew the money he was saving would be of good use one day. He had grown fond of the powerful machine his dad possessed. Aside from Rich and his belated mother, there wasn't anything else in the world Treacherous loved more then his twelfth-birthday present and bikes. One particular night, while dreaming, Treacherous was awakened out of his sleep at the sound of the loud *boom* that came from the downstairs. He had no idea what it was and hopped out of his bed to see what was going on. As he got closer to the stairs he heard the many different voices yelling from below. Not knowing what to expect, Treacherous doubled back and snatched up his twelfth-birthday present. Upon tiptoeing down the stairs he noticed his father sprawled out over the living-room floor. The first thought that came to his mind was they were being robbed, but he cancelled that thought once he saw the men wearing the blue jackets that bore the letters *FBI* in big bright yellow letters on the back. Treacherous couldn't imagine why the FBI could be after his father, who he had thought to be a local stickup man who occasionally was a hired gun. His dad wasn't a coke pusher or dope dealer, let alone some type of kingpin. To Treacherous's knowledge, only the big-time gangstas and the Mafia got knocked by the feds, and although his father was all gangster, he was small-time. Or at least that's what Treacherous believed. He thought that his father's rep only extended as far as their own hood. Had he known the true depths of his father's reputation, he would have known why the feds were at his home in the middle of the night. Realizing he had his twelfth-birthday present still out in his hand, he tiptoed back up the stairs with the intention of hiding it. He knew that it was just a matter of time before the feds came up. As soon as he reached the top, he heard one of the agents tell another to go check on the boy. Knowing he was "the boy," Treacherous played possum as the agent walked into his room.

"Treacherous," the agent called, shaking him by the shoulder. Treacherous was surprised the man had known his name. He opened his eyes as if he had just been awakened out of a deep sleep. "My name is Agent Grimes. Don't worry, I'm not going to hurt you. I just need you to come with me," the agent instructed. "I'll wait in the hall for you to get dressed."

"Where's my dad?" Treacherous asked, already knowing.

"Your dad's downstairs. You'll see him shortly, but for now I need you to put something on and come with me." Treacherous knew he had no other choice but to comply. He got up and slipped on his clothes.

"That's a good boy," the agent stated, seeing Treacherous was dressed. He had been through situations with other children in the past and things did not go as smoothly. The agent escorted Treacherous downstairs. When he reached the living room, his father was nowhere to be found.

"Where's my dad?" Treacherous asked a second time. "I thought you said he was down here?"

"Take it easy, young fella," Agent Grimes replied, thinking he had now spoken too soon. "Some of my friends escorted your dad to another place, not too far from where I'm going to be escorting you."

Other agents attended to their duties while Agent Grimes continued to pacify Treacherous.

He was not naive, nor was he a dummy. He knew his father had been arrested; he just didn't know what for.

"Where are you taking me?" he asked.

"You're going to spend the remainder of the night with some friends of mine and someone will pick you up in the morning. They'll explain everything to you about your dad, all right?"

Treacherous remained silent. He couldn't believe what was happening. His head was spinning and his mind was moving a mile a minute. What could his father have done so bad that would bring the feds to their house?

"I got it," the agent shouted to the others. When Treacherous looked, the agent was coming from out of his father's bedroom with an oversized green army duffel bag. Treacherous had never seen the bag before and wondered what it contained. One by one they all congratulated him.

Treacherous was lost. He had no clue why the agents began to celebrate, but whatever the reason, he knew it was in the duffel bag.

Chapter Seven

"Good morning, Treacherous," the lady greeted as she entered the small-spaced room. "My name is Ms. Lyles. I'm with the child welfare and social services department. Do you know what that is?" she asked.

Treacherous did not respond. He knew exactly who the woman worked for. She was dressed the same way the white women who came in his neighborhood to remove kids from their parents dressed. He refused to answer any questions or cooperate with the woman, who reeked of cheap perfume, stale cigarettes, and strong coffee. Treacherous knew better than to answer anything, especially when there was a strong possibility if he did it could hurt his father's situation. He had no way of knowing it was over for his dad no matter what he did or didn't say. The only thing Treacherous learned was that his father had been arrested and taken into custody on armed robbery and attempted murder charges, from what he gathered based on the questions the lady had asked him. She would begin her sentences with, "Were you aware that your father was this or your father was . . ." often switching up the same questions by saying, "Did your father ever talk to you about . . ." or "You could really help your father by telling me about . . ."

After refusing to answer the lady's questions and seeing that she wasn't getting anywhere, Ms. Lyles informed Treacherous she would be placing him in a residence in Norfolk. The Department of Child Services housed young kids until they found placement.

Even before Treacherous arrived at the all-boys home, he had already made up his mind about what he was going to do. The social worker escorted him to the elderly, heavyset black woman and left him there until his case was reviewed and placement was made—at least that's what the social worker thought. No sooner than she pulled off Treacherous was out the back door in the wind, going unnoticed. Treacherous was out of breath as he ran nonstop from the house twenty minutes straight until he felt he had put enough distance between himself and the boys home. He had no money in his pockets and all he had was the clothes on his back, so his first stop was where he knew he could go to change that. When he entered the house, Treacherous shot straight to his bedroom. He had 120 dollars stashed in a Nike shoe box under his bed that he had saved from his collections at school, along with his twelfth-birthday present. His intentions were to gather as many clothes as he could, then make his way back to his old neighborhood, where he felt the most comfortable. He had no family to turn to or any friends. All he ever had was his father, who had been taken away from him. Treacherous knew he was officially on his own. The reason for his father had taught and instilled in him all that he had had became clear at that very moment for Treacherous. It was for survival. In that instant Treacherous realized that his father had foreseen the day a long time ago, and knew it was time to put all he was taught into action.

Chapter Eight

After collecting as much of his belongings as he could, Treacherous could see the cab he had called to pick him up one block over from his house. Treacherous had to break the back window and climb through in order to get inside the house, which was pitch-black. Treacherous assumed the agents had turned off the lights before they secured the home. He remembered his father had a big suitcase he kept in his closet and figured he could pack his things in there. Finding the suitcase, Treacherous decided to search his father's dresser drawers for anything of value, and to his surprise he found a stack of money in a gold money clip and a few pieces of jewelry. The agents must have overlooked this, he thought, as he slipped the clip off the money and counted it before shoving both the cash and jewelry in his pockets. The total of the money was 750 dollars. That was the most paper he had ever held in his hands at one time in his life. With the 120 dollars he had upstairs, that brought him to almost 900 dollars in cash.

The jewelry consisted of a gold nugget watch, a Rolex presidential with diamond bezels, a thick rolled-gold link bracelet with a chain to match, and another chain that was a solid rope. He had never seen his father wear any of his jewelry or any other jewelry for that matter, so he knew his dad had robbed someone for it. He continued to rummage through the drawers, this time coming across two more items that would become useful to him. They were his father's two .38s, which he had carried at all times. Treacherous grabbed them up and tucked them both up under his shirt like he had seen his father do a million times before leaving the house. He then went upstairs and got his possessions, then snuck back out the way he'd snuck in. When the taxi arrived, Treacherous hopped in.

"Where to?" the driver asked

"Tidewater Park housing projects."

All the Tidewater Park project heads saw Treacherous approaching and hit him with long-hard stares. Treacherous wondered why everyone was looking at him as if he were a ghost. He had ditched his suitcase a block away in a trash can before he had approached the projects he was all too familiar with, careful not to draw suspicion, but he kept the two trey-eights and his twelfth-birthday present on him just as a safety precaution since he had a pocketful of dough. Tidewater Park projects fiends were the worse rock stars and dopeheads in the area he knew, so he wasn't trying to leave himself open to get jacked out there, contributing to some junkie's filling his lungs or his veins with poisonous drugs.

He walked through his old hood meeting each individual's eyes, returning their stares. In some eyes he saw admiration and concern, while in others he saw pure hatred, and for the life of him he couldn't figure out why he was being grilled the way he was as a sense of silence swept the projects. Not once did he break his stare. He was taught to look a person dead in their eyes when he talked to them or they wanted to play the staring game. He was told by his father that to break the stare was a sign of weakness or surrender. Instead of Treacherous giving in to the stares, each man dropped their eyes as he walked through. Some tried to maintain their murderous grills, but they were no match for Treacherous's stone face.

Treacherous had no idea what his intentions were when he reached the projects. He just knew this was where he felt most comfortable and safe, even though Tidewater Park projects was far from a safe place to be. As he walked through, Treacherous noticed the old-timer everyone referred to as O.G., sitting in front of an apartment. At the same time O.G. spotted Treacherous and motioned for him. Treacherous had observed his father talking to the old-timer before and noticed him leaving out of the apartment a few times when he was coming home from school. Based on those two facts he decided to see what O.G. wanted. Everyone watched as Treacherous walked in O.G.'s direction. Then, like a stopwatch that had been restarted, everyone resumed what they were doing, knowing O.G. would school Richie Gunz's kid. This was the first time Treacherous had been in O.G.'s presence up-close. He studied the old-timer. O.G.'s hair was like a silver lining. Its grays were permed and slightly wavy, neatly slicked to the back. His eyes were like black pearls and beady, Treacherous noticed as he stared into them, similar to his father's, he thought. O.G.'s face looked like stone. Treacherous could see the muscles in O.G.'s clean-shaved face each time he chewed on the straw he had partially hanging out of his mouth. O.G.'s gold tooth glistened every other second as he chewed on the straw. Treacherous recalled how his father often chewed on straws and how Rich's face was also stone-looking, but not as much as O.G.'s. Treacherous couldn't help but to notice the similarities of O.G.'s demeanor and that of his dad's.

"Li'l Treach, what you doin' around here?" asked O.G. His voice was a raspy and low toned. Treacherous leaned in, not knowing whether O.G. really spoke so low or was trying to speak for his ears only.

Treacherous detected the concern in O.G.'s question, but didn't know why the man was so interested in anything about him. He decided to play it safe until he found out O.G.'s motives behind his question. Rich had taught him well. *Trust no one,* he heard his father say in his mind.

"I just came to visit the old neighborhood and see my friends," Treacherous replied with skepticism. O.G. laughed to himself at Treacherous's weak game he was spitting at him, but he respected it, though. His father had definitely taught him well, thought O.G., but one fatal mistake he made was by telling a lie and O.G. had seen right through it. O.G. had watched as Rich raised Treacherous and knew all there was to know about him. What Treacherous didn't know was that Rich got what little parenting skills from him, and O.G. was actually Treacherous's godfather. Had he had enough time he would have taken his godson to school on "game," but time was not in their favor at this point in time.

"Boy, you ain't got no friends." O.G. laughed. "Your old man ain't let you have none, and in case you wonderin' how I know that, it's because I'm the one that told him not to let you have none, 'cause you never know when you might have to do something to one of these lame-ass turkeys out here. That way you won't have no regrets or remorse when you do." Treacherous became wide eyed.

Here was this old man who sat in front of him quoting the same words used by his father. There was no way this man could have known that unless he was close to his father, Treacherous concluded, so he was eager to hear more from the old-timer.

"Why'd my dad trust you, he didn't trust no one?" he asked

O.G. snickered at the question. "Listen, Treach, we ain't got time for no twenty questions or no history class, 'cause it's hot out here right now. One thing you need to know, though, is that I raised your dad in the game. He used to run for me and do other little odd jobs, you dig? Then when your momma died I helped Rich raise you, but I played the backfield 'cause you was his kid to raise and I didn't want to come between that. He came to me for advice and I gave it, that simple. He made me your godfather and that's why I'm pullin' you up right now."

Treacherous listened as O.G. talked taking it all in.

"Right now those people are looking for you. One of the local snitches said you ran away from social services," O.G. said as he laughed. "I don't blame you, but it's just a matter of time 'fore one of these jealous-ass niggas drop a dime and let them know you around here, so you can't stay too long."

Treacherous reflected and it all made sense why he had received all the stares. Although he knew his father's charges, he was still in the dark about what really happened and he knew O.G. could shed some light on the situation.

"Why the feds got my pops?"

O.G. looked at him, puzzled, but then understood why Rich had kept this from him, but it was time for him to know.

"Your old man robbed a bank," O.G. started. "Matter of fact, he robbed a couple of banks," O.G. continued as a smirk came across his face the way a proud father smiles when hearing of his son's accomplishments.

"But this last bank he hit he shot a couple of people and took a lot of money from them people. When he moved y'all up out of the projects and into that house the streets started talkin, 'cause the streets is always watching. I don't know who or how they got onto your old man, but my guess is once they got the word they put a tail on him. A lot of them muthafuckas up in here didn't like your daddy, but they was scared to death of him, so to see him off the streets is a blessing to them. Now they can sleep better at night and eat more because your pops was shakin' them little punks down left and right, even after he robbed that bank. I told him he didn't have to keep robbing, but that's what he liked to do, that was his first love, so I couldn't get him to stop that easy. He had given me two hundred and fifty Gs from his take and told me he had made out with a million-two. If I hadn't read it in the papers saying they confiscated over nine hundred grand from out of his house to this day I wouldn't have believed it. I don't know how he pulled it off 'cause he never told me, but he did it."

As O.G. spoke, Treacherous realized for the first time in his life that his father was not just some small-time gangsta, he was as big as some of the all-time greats like Jesse James, Dillinger, Baby Face Nelson, Pretty Boy Floyd, and even Clyde. He wondered if his moms had been Bonnie. Treacherous had never been more proud than he was right then of his father, the man he would one day become.

"How your pockets lookin'? You good on bread?" O.G. asked.

"Yeah, I'm straight," answered Treacherous, thinking about the 800 dollars and some change he had on him.

"A'ight, well, if you ever need anything don't hesitate to ask. Don't be proud. I know your old man taught you a closed mouth don't get fed, but if you can't make it here that ain't no need for you to starve, if you ain't got it and you need it then you gots to take it from somebody who has it. I'm giving it to you like I gave it to your old man when he was your age. You got a piece on you?" asked O.G.

"Yeah, I got three. The one my pops brought me and the two he carried," Treacherous stated boldly.

"Good, that's good, then you set. Where you stayin'?"

"Wherever I lay my head," Treacherous responded.

O.G. wished that he had sons like Treacherous and Rich, who he felt were built for the mean streets. He viewed his own two sons as cowards, both who he had lost to the streets. In spite of the big age difference he and O.G. felt just as his dad, Treacherous was cut from the same cloth as himself, which was that of a gangster.

"Look here, take this key, I gotta a little stash crib that I keep in case of emergencies around the corner. You can stay there until you get situated."

Treacherous took the key.

"Thanks O.G.," he said.

"Call me G.F. O.G. is for these cats in the streets. I'm your godfather."

"A'ight G.F.," Treacherous corrected.

"Go ahead and get up outta here and be safe," he said, giving Treacherous dap with a closed fist. He was a man who showed little emotions, which was why he never hugged or shook hands. He was truly an old-school gangsta.

Treacherous left the projects, caught up in his own thoughts, paying no mind to the dudes he had been playing the staring game with when he first arrived at his old neighborhood. Just as Treacherous reached the end of the projects, his thoughts were interrupted.

"Treacherous Freeman," someone blared out. Before Treacherous had time to focus on the unfamiliar voice, he was swarmed by two unmarked police cars. It didn't take a genius to figure out what had happened. Someone had dropped a dime on him and informed the cops of his whereabouts. Treacherous was now boxed in. He had little room to think or react. He contemplated making a run for it but quickly x-ed that option out.

"Just stay right there, son," one of the officers ordered, cautiously making his way over toward Treacherous, whose heart rate increased. He knew in a situation such as the one he was in he was doomed. Treacherous stood there with hands in his pockets, watching the officer closely as two more exited the other police car.

"Son, let me see your hands," the officer calmly stated. "Slowly take them out one at a time, for your safety and mine, all right, buddy?"

Treacherous could already see the outcome of his predicament. He knew he had been caught in the wrong place at the wrong time and there was nothing he could do about it. One by one Treacherous slowly slid his hands out of his jacket pockets. Relieved, but still cautious, the officer continued to approach Treacherous while his partners did the same from opposite sides. Everyone in the projects watched from a distance as the police drew in.

"Son, you do know why we're here, right?" the officer questioned, receiving no reply. "There are some people who are concerned about your well-being. They gave us a call and said you ran away from the children's home. We're just here to escort you back, that's all, son," the officer continued in a subtle tone. He had been a police officer for ten years. Something about Treacherous's demeanor made him uneasy.

"Now, all of this can be over in just a few minutes, but I'm gonna need you to help me out here." Treacherous continued to stand there in silence, listening to the officer attempting to con him. He already knew his fate.

"I'm going to need you to step over to the car. Let me pat you down, then my friends and I will escort you back to the house." By then, the other two officers were positioned behind Treacherous, prepared for the worse. They were immune to bad-reputation housing projects from responding to incidents at some point in their career. On many occasions calls resulted in them having to use physical force or draw their weapons, so they didn't treat the situation any different. Treacherous walked over to the nearest police car.

"Thanks, son. I appreciate your cooperation," the officer stated genuinely.

"Stop calling me *son*. You're not my father," Treacherous spit. It was the first words he had said since the police had closed him in. The officer was taken aback by Treacherous's words. For a split second, he had the urge to pull his gun, but when he saw Treacherous place his hands on the hood of the car, he disregarded the urge.

"No problem, young fella," the officer corrected. Instantly he began patting down Treacherous. "Don't move," he yelled, quickly drawing his weapon. His tone triggered his colleagues and they too now drew their weapons. The onlookers in the neighborhood began to draw in closer to see what was happening.

"Everybody back up," one of the other officers yelled to the crowd that was now forming.

"Son, get on the ground. Now!" the officer ordered him.

Calmly, Treacherous complied. He could hear sirens in the distance. He counted three pair of feet as he lay on the pavement. The officers now had him secured. The officer who ordered Treacherous on the ground discovered he had more on his person then he would have ever imagined. Initially Treacherous knew he would have been taken back to the group home, but with the three guns, along with the money and stolen jewelry, he knew he would be paying a visit to the youth house. Just as he figured, they found his weapons along with the rest of the contents in his pockets and began handcuffing him.

Treacherous knew if his father could see him he would be disappointed. He made a mental promise to himself that as long as he lived the police would never catch him ever again like this.

Chapter Nine

Norfolk Detention Center was jammed with young adolescents and juvenile delinquents. It took no time for Treacherous to find position and gain status up in the juvenile jail for young boys and girls. He had been charged with illegal possession of firearms and receiving stolen property. When he went to court after three days the caseworker he remembered questioning him was there. After she spoke the judge called Treach a menace to society and a threat to the community and remanded him in detention until he reached the age of eighteen. To all the other kids who only had to serve a couple weeks, months, or a year or two, what Treacherous had was a juvenile life sentence, so they all respected him for his time. In addition to that, they had discovered that the man they had read about in the newspapers and some knew of and respected, was Treacherous's father. What they thought about Treacherous made him no difference. His only concern was serving the five and a half years in confinement, and how he would pay society back for stripping him of his father as well as his freedom. Some kids learned their lessons and went home better than they came in. Treach had never committed a crime in his life, but was being condemned and punished for what his father had done, and he was angry at the judicial system, so instead of learning any lessons and going home and becoming a productive part of society, he vowed he would leave up out of there worse than when he entered.

Four years went by and Treacherous grew both physically and mentally. If he wasn't doing push-ups or dips he was reading a book. He had gotten his GED two years prior and began to teach himself by acquiring more knowledge through the books that were available to him, which were mostly white historical books. Treacherous wasn't fortunate to have someone on the outside to send him any good books, but there was one kid who had gotten in a bunch of books by some black authors and he offered Treacherous the opportunity to read them. Treacherous enjoyed reading, especially while he was on room-lockdown from fighting. Treacherous had a total of twenty-nine fights in the four-year span he had been in the detention center, and won every last one of them. Whenever Treacherous would get locked down, the kid would slide a book under the door for him. Treacherous had read all of the books by Donald Goines and Iceberg Slim over and over until he practically knew them by heart. He had his Goines favorites like the Kenyatta sequels and *Black Girl Lost*, but his all- time favorite was *Black Gangster*. *Pimp* was his favorite of Iceberg Slim, along with *Long White Con*. It was through these books he had become more educated with the many aspects of the game. He realized, through the books he read, whether you were a pimp, player, con, drug dealer, or a gangsta, you were still a hustler and you only had two choices: Either you go out there and go hard by making it, or you go hard by taking it. From that day forward Treacherous knew what he was going to do upon his release. It was in his blood, he rationalized.

"What's up, Treach?" was all he heard as he made his way to the breakfast line. Treacherous had grown accustomed to the type of attention he received. The detention center had been his home for the past few years and he practically ran it. He knew some spoke out of respect while others out of fear. But either way, Treacherous gave none of them the time of day. He was a loner by nature, and that's the way he liked it. Treacherous had just gotten off room restrictions after being locked down for twenty-one days when he entered the dayroom. He was eighteen months short of getting his release and decided that he would chill this time, since his time was quickly coming to an end. As he got his breakfast and sat down he noticed the young females who had been released from the girls' side to eat. Over the years young girls had come and gone, none really catching Treacherous, who compared all females to his mother, but as he zeroed in on the five girls, two black, one white, and one Hispanic-looking one of the black girls, stood out from the rest. She looked out of place, but if he looked hard enough you could see the toughness in her eyes. Treacherous thought she favored his mother slightly. This was the first time he had ever thought someone was worthy of even being compared.

The medium-height, light-brown–skinned girl noticed Treacherous staring at her as their eyes met. She had only been in the detention center for ten days but throughout that short period of time she had practically seen all the guys that had been in there, most of them trying to talk to her, but after the first few days of being unsuccessful they began to view her as stuck-up. She had heard stories about a kid named Treacherous who had been in detention for four years and stayed on lockdown for fighting. She was told that he ran Tidewater Detention House. Now, laying eyes on Treacherous had her confident he was the one who the girls spoke about, even before the other girls who knew of him had confirmed it.

While everyone else sat at the tables grouped up, Treacherous sat alone. It had been that way for years now. Apparently, no one told the new girl that. She headed toward the table where he was sitting. Treacherous saw the girl heading his way and stopped eating his cereal. When she reached his table he looked up at her. Closer up, she favored his mother's picture a little more, he thought.

"Is this seat taken?" she asked with the deepest but softest voice he had ever heard from a female.

Instead of answering, Treacherous shook his head. The girl sat down. Everyone looked as the new girl sat with him. All the boys in the detention center were jealous while the girls were envious. Even the staff was in disbelief. No one had bothered to inform the new girl that Treacherous liked to eat alone and expected him to blow up on her, but to their surprise he didn't.

Treacherous continued eating his cereal as the girl fumbled, trying to open her milk. She hoped that her nervousness in Treacherous's presence didn't show on the outside because on the inside she was a nervous wreck. She had never met a guy who reeked of strength and commanded respect. She saw how he had the entire facility walking on eggshells. Her now ex-boyfriend, who was the reason why she was in the detention center in the first place, had been the leader of his block but he was not respected or feared the way she felt he should have been. She was only fifteen but her ex was nineteen. As sharp as she thought she was, she couldn't believe how naive she had been when it came to him, and now she was sitting up in jail for him.

The new girl continued to fight with the milk carton as Treacherous watched her out of the corner of his eye as he ate. He was tempted to help her but he just couldn't bring himself to. That was not his style. He was a gangsta, and gangstas kept it gangsta at all times. The new girl thought she had the difficult milk carton licked, but as she peeled the flaps open, the milk slipped out of her hands. "Oh shit, my bad," she chimed, seeing the milk had spilled over the table toward Treacherous. He jumped up just as the milk began pouring in his lap. Everyone saw the commotion and turned their attention toward Treacherous and the new girl.

"Clumsy-ass chick," Treacherous shouted as he brushed the milk off the front of his jumper.

The girl was about to apologize for her mistake until she was interrupted by the words that came out of Treacherous's mouth.

"What? Fuck you," she retorted. "It was a mistake. Who the fuck you calling clumsy?"

All the other girls and guys looked at the new girl as if she had lost her mind. The other kids were sure now Treacherous was going to knock the new girl's teeth down her throat for the blatant disrespect. They had never heard anyone take the tone with Treacherous the way the new girl had done.

Treacherous looked at the girl as if her words lashed at him. Before he could even do or say anything, staff ran and jumped between the two of them.

"Mr. Freeman, please go over there," one of the staff members requested, pleading with him while the other staff tried to escort the new girl out of the dining area.

Treacherous knew why they were handling him in such a manner. On several occasions throughout his stay at the detention center, Treacherous had become untamable whenever altercations arose with him and another resident. This was Treacherous's first time ever getting into a situation with a female. What the staff could not have known was no matter what the girl had said to him, Treacherous would never put his hands on her. He did as he was told and backed up as he watched the new girl carry on.

"Get your fucking hands off me, bitch," she screamed as she punched one of the female staffers in the midsection.

Another one tried to calm her down, only to be met with the new girl's fist to her jaw, putting her to the floor. That's when two male staff grabbed her from behind. Even they had a hard time with the feisty and rowdy girl.

"Why y'all catering to that mu'fucka', I didn't do shit!" she yelled as she kicked and scratched all the way out the dayroom.

Everyone laughed at the performance. Everyone except Treacherous. He had never met a female like her and admired her tenacity. She fought for what she believed in and said what others wished they could have said to him. Treacherous reflected on something he had read in a book: *If you don't stand for something then you'll fall for anything.* He knew the girl was only standing up for what she believed in. After everything had died down, Treacherous went back to his room where he felt most comfortable, picked up a book, and began to read. He couldn't help but think about the girl who resembled his mother, who just caused so much trouble. Based on the stories his father had told him about her, he could see the new girl also shared his mother's fire.

By lunch Treacherous had overheard how the staff had locked down the girl for forty-five days for the earlier incident.

He had also learned how much time she was serving by overhearing someone saying she was going to have a rough sixteen months in the institution. While eating lunch, he came across the girl's name from the discussion the other girls were having at the table across from him. Treacherous thought the name Teflon to be peculiar for a girl, but then again, who was he to talk about names? His father had given him the reason behind his name and wondered what had possessed the girl's parents to give her such a name.

Chapter Ten

Teflon laid across the bed with her arms folded, locked inside the little six-by-nine room. Out of all the places in the world she could be, she wondered how she landed herself in this hellhole, but she knew the answer to that: From dealing with a man, or let her tell it, a little boy who thought he was the man. That, and being in the wrong place at the wrong time.

All her life, as far back as she could remember, Teflon had to be on her grind and had to struggle looking after herself. The one time she let her guard down, thinking she had found true love, and let someone dictate how she should live and pump her up with all types of lies, selling her dreams and giving her false hope—that's when her life changed drastically for the worse. The result was Teflon being sentenced to sixteen months in Norfolk Detention Center for possession with intent and aggravated assault with a weapon. Teflon didn't mind being charged with the assault because she was guilty of that.

She smiled as she replayed the incident the day she was taken into custody. Teflon and her then boyfriend were just coming home after having an enjoyable dinner and evening at a popular restaurant in downtown Norfolk. As she unlocked her home and opened the door, she didn't think anything of the darkness as they entered the two-bedroom condo her boyfriend had purchased for her as a birthday present under the table, in her name. As she reached for the light to illuminate her domain, she and her boyfriend were met with badges, guns, and a barrage of yelling. Both her and her boyfriend did as were told and hit the ground quick and fast. When the officer approached her and her boyfriend with the packaged drugs and asked the unforgettable question of whose drugs it was, Teflon—looking over to her boyfriend, confident he would step up to the plate, something he had always preached—she could not believe her ears. "That shit ain't mine. I don't live here. I'm just visiting my girl." You would have thought he was Denzel Washington the way words came out of his mouth. Her now ex-boyfriend would always remember how he had did her dirty every time he looked in the mirror and saw the scar on his face that ran from the side of his eye down to the corner of his mouth, compliments of Teflon's blade, which she kept in her mouth at all times, the way she used to see her mother do before they parted. Far from being a dummy, seeing that the fix was in, Teflon spit the razor into her hand just as quick as any veteran on Rikers Island and caught her ex across the face, good enough to send him to the hospital for 150 stitches, known as a buck fifty. The police maced Teflon with pepper spray to subdue her and carried her off to detention while they took her ex to the hospital.

He was charged with the drugs in the house as well but posted bail. Because she refused to tell who the drugs really belonged to and her ex had already given his statement, he beat his case and Teflon wore the weight. She couldn't bring herself to snitch on somebody. It just wasn't in her blood. She took the sixteen months they gave her and maintained her integrity and self-respect, compromising neither of the two. Neither of her parents were ever really there for her or told her anything to prepare her for the life that lay ahead of her, but what she knew about them both, she assumed they played the game fair, each playing their role and position.

As she lay in the bed she couldn't help but think about the guy named Treacherous. It wasn't her intention to beef with him the way she had, but he had caught her vein. She had an issue with the way people talked to her, males in particular. Her mother had instilled that inside of her and there was no exception to the rule. Besides, all that was built up inside of Teflon for her ex was released and directed toward him. Teflon realized she wasn't even mad at him. She had no right to be because she barely knew him, other than what she had heard about him. *He must think I'm crazy,* she thought as she dwelled on the situation. Why was she so concerned about what he thought about her? She had no clue, but she promised herself when her forty-five-day room restriction was up she would step to him again, only with a different approach. Teflon laid back and closed her eyes. Images of her childhood haunted her, invading her mind as she slipped into a trance and began to relive her past.

Chapter Eleven

"Ho, I keep telling you I don't give a fuck about that little bastard. What you better do is get your ass out there and get me my paper before I stomp a mud hole on your funky ass," Popsicle barked.

Pearl held back her tears. Her eyes were filled with flames as she shot Popsicle a look of disgust. Ever since she had told him four years ago she was pregnant with his child he had been denying it, calling their daughter a bastard. But Pearl knew Teflon was his no matter how many tricks she turned. She always kept track of the times and days she and Popsicle made love. He was totally against her having the baby and on many occasions he even tried to stomp her into a miscarriage when she was four months, but was unsuccessful. That was why she named her daughter Teflon, on account of her surviving despite Popsicle's attempts. After a while he left Pearl alone when he saw she continued to hump all the way through her pregnancy, and after not waiting for the required six weeks after she delivered to end. The older Teflon got, the lazier Pearl became in the streets, and Popsicle just wasn't having it. He had invested a lot of time, energy, money, and pimp game into her to have her turn into a square broad on him. Before he allowed that to happen he would kill her and the bastard child.

Pearl was a runaway teen from New York who wanted to become a model and explore the world. She definitely looked the part, but her biggest downfall was she was as green as a pool-table carpet when it came to the streets and couldn't recognize game when Popsicle rolled up on her in his cream-colored Cadillac with a beige vinyl top and interior to match. To Pearl, Popsicle was the best thing since a hot comb with his fly ride, sharp threads, and slick tongue. Popsicle was fourteen years her senior and a pimp from out of Pittsburgh. Using his pimp skills and taking advantage of her greenness, it was as easy as taking candy from a baby for Popsicle to manipulate Pearl into proving her love for him by selling her body to help support and contribute to his expensive tastes. Back then she would have done anything for Popsicle because she was young and in love, but as she got older, the streets had hardened her. She had gotten a heavy dose of reality the ten years she had been out in the streets, and the only thing she had to show for it was a child whose father didn't claim her, but little Teflon was her pride and joy. She had to tried to stop hooking when Teflon began getting older because that was not a part of her life she wanted her daughter to see, but being a woman of limited skills, this was all she felt she could do to feed and put clothes on her and her child's back.

Popsicle had shattered her dreams of becoming a model when he gamed her into becoming a prostitute. Ever since he had taken her from New York to Pittsburgh, then eventually to Ventura, Pearl's life had been a world of turmoil. She had been pulling back from the streets lately to spend more time with her daughter, but hearing the hostility in Popsicle's voice as he yelled at her, Pearl knew her vacation from the ho stroll had come to an end. She knew if she didn't get back out there full- time and bring a nice chunk of change home to Popsicle, he would try to hurt both her and Teflon, but she had no one to attend to her daughter, who was far too young to be left alone, so Pearl was faced with a dilemma.

"Daddy, I wanna make some money for you, baby, but who gonna look after my daughter?" said Pearl, carefully choosing her words, not wanting to anger Popsicle any more than he already was by referring to Teflon as their child.

Popsicle recognized the game Pearl was trying to run on him. That was the first time she had excluded him from the little bastard kid since she had her. He laughed at the thought of Pearl trying to stroke him the way she tried. At first, he was going to back-hand the taste out of her mouth for even thinking that she could run that weak-ass game on him, but he knew that she was immune to his smacks, punches, kicks, and occasional pimp hanger game, so he decided to hurt her in another way.

"Ho, don't be worrying about this little bastard. Just take your ass out there and get my paper straight. I got her, and when you come back up in here, everything better be intact. I'll be here waitin' with your damn trick baby," Popsicle stated.

It was unusual for him to be so quick to help her with anything—let alone with their child, she thought—but Pearl shook her notion off and looked at it as him just wanting her to go out and make his money. Had she not still been in love with Popsicle after all of these years and felt he still had her best interest at heart, she would've questioned and pondered his intent and motives. But in her mind, when it came to Popsicle, Pearl was still that young, naive seventeen-year-old he had found on the streets of New York years ago.

Teflon watched as her mother transformed right before her very eyes, exchanging her lounge-around-the house outfit, into a red tube top, black leather miniskirt, and black leather knee-high pumps, and where her mother's hair was short- cropped and naturally black, it was replaced with a long, blond Chinese-bob wig. She smiled at how pretty her mommy looked as Pearl put on her blue eye shadow, red lipstick, and some blush to highlight her high cheekbones.

After she checked herself out in the mirror, Pearl transferred all her necessities from out of a green purse into a red shoulder bag, which would be the final accessory to her outfit. Pearl felt good. She admired herself in the mirror: the way her tight-fitted outfit hugged her body, as she hiked her skirt up more to become more revealing. She was dressed to kill and knew she would turn a lot of heads and a lot of tricks when she stepped on the scene tonight. Before she left, she walked over to Teflon.

"Baby girl, Mommy gotta go to work, but I'll be back soon. Mr. Popsicle gonna watch you while I'm gone, so I want you to be on your best behavior, you hear me?" Pearl said to her daughter.

"Um-hmm," answered Teflon in a childlike manner.

"Good. When I come back I'll bring some cookies and ice cream with me. I know you'll like that, right?"

Teflon's eyes lit up at the sound of her favorite junk food being mentioned. If she intended to give Mr. Popsicle any trouble before, she had now changed her mind.

"Okay, now give your mommy a kiss and hug."

Teflon reached out and embraced her mother. Pearl hugged Teflon with all her might. Pearl didn't want to let her daughter go, but she knew she had a job to do. Besides, she did not want to hear Popsicle's mouth. Pearl took one last look at herself and got into what she called her "ho zone." It took all she had inside of her to release Teflon. Teflon did not want to let go of her mother, either. Pearl gave Teflon one last hug.

"Let Mommy get out of here, baby," she said.

Teflon let go, and Pearl stood up and brushed the wrinkles out of her skirt and adjusted her top. The whole time Popsicle stood there watching the scene between mother and daughter. He felt the child had made Pearl weak, but after tonight that would all change, he told himself.

"I love you, Teffy."

"I love you too, Mommy."

With that, Pearl made a beeline to the door. She looked at Popsicle before she left.

"Go on, ho, 'fo ya ass be in tears and you fuck ya makeup all up. I said I got her," said Popsicle.

Pearl shot him a half smile. She knew if she stayed any longer and looked at her daughter she would in fact break down and cry, and change her plans to hit the streets, but then she would have to deal with Popsicle. With that thought she was out the door.

Teflon stared at the man her mother always referred to as Popsicle. She had seen him come and go her whole life. She was not old enough to understand what type of relationship her mother and this man had, but she had heard her mother say that she was his child too, on a few occasions, and she remembered how upset he would get at her mother whenever she said it to him. She didn't know what the words meant at the time when Popsicle would call her mother *ho* and *bitch* or refer to her as *bastard*, but Teflon knew that they were not good words and wondered why the man would talk to her mother and about her like that. In spite of all the yelling and bad words he used, Teflon was not afraid of Popsicle, which was why she walked over to him.

Popsicle was in the kitchen mixing up a concoction when Teflon approached him. Hearing her little footsteps caused him to turn around.

"Mr. Popsicle, are you my daddy?" asked Teflon.

Popsicle was thrown by the question. He didn't think that a child so young would ask such a thing.

"Yeah, baby girl, I'm your daddy," he said as gentle as any father could.

"So why you always call my mommy bad names when she say that?"

Popsicle laughed to himself. He couldn't believe how smart the little girl was and wondered could she have really been his kid, but immediately dismissed the thought. Even if she was his kid it wouldn't make a difference. He would never claim to have fathered a child by a whore. That's what Pearl was to him. He knew he had to answer her questions if he wanted her to trust him.

"That's how me and your mommy play. She knows I don't mean it. I love her."

Hearing that melted Teflon's six-year-old heart. She had never heard anyone say that they loved her mother besides her, and that won her over.

"She loves you too, Daddy," replied Teflon, hugging him by the knees.

Popsicle disregarded what Teflon had said to him. His coldheartedness overpowered his conscience.

"Baby girl, Daddy made you something," Popsicle said as he grabbed a glass and handed to her. "Drink this."

Teflon looked at the glass. Chocolate milk was one of her favorite desserts but it looked darker than the regular chocolate milk she was used to her mother making her.

"Daddy, what is it?" she asked innocently.

"It's a special drink. Daddy drinks it all the time," Popsicle said. Teflon took the glass and examined it before she attempted to drink the liquid. She had no way of knowing the drink consisted of rat poison, Visine, and ammonia, mixed with milk and Nestlé Quik. Popsicle was becoming impatient with Teflon's examination. He was tempted to grab her by the neck and force the poison down her throat, but he knew that foul play could easily be detected if he did it that way, so he had to let things play out by themselves. Satisfied with her examination, Teflon began raising the glass to her lips, only to be stopped by her mother's voice.

***

Pearl began walking the streets of Portsmouth en route to her normal stomping grounds. This was where she usually made her most money. As she got a few blocks down from her apartment her mind began to drift. Something wasn't sitting right with her; she just couldn't pinpoint what it was, but she could feel it. Out of force of habit she began looking around to see if she was being followed or something of the sort. Being out on the streets for so long, her senses and awareness had become keen. She had become accustomed to staying on point when she was out there running them. Paranoia swept through her entire body like a jolt of lightning, and she began to get the chills. For the life of her, Pearl couldn't figure out why she was feeling this way. The last time she had felt this way was when Popsicle had tried to make her lose her baby. It took her two weeks before she had hit the streets again. At the thought of the beating Popsicle had put on her over four years ago, Pearl began to wonder why she had agreed to leave her pride and joy in his care, then it all came together like a Ku Klux Klan meeting. Popsicle intended to hurt her baby. Pearl immediately turned around and began running back to her apartment, which was only five blocks away. Her mother's intuition began to kick in full-speed as she frantically raced back to the apartment. She would never be able to live with herself if something was to happen to Teflon. She told herself if one hair was touched on her daughter, Popsicle would not live either.

Her high-heel pumps clicked and clanked the way a tap dancer's shoes does against the pavement. Her strides were long and athletic, and before she knew it she had arrived back at her apartment in record-breaking time, without even being out of breath. She chalked it up as a mother's love because in the midst of a child's danger, superhuman strength is given to a parent to aid them. She ran up the three flights, skipping every other step and reached her apartment. When she opened up the door, she saw Popsicle standing in front of her daughter in the kitchen area while Teflon stood there with a glass in her hands.

"Tef," she shouted, causing Teflon to withdraw the glass from her lips.

"Mommy! You back," Teflon yelled, both happy and surprised to be seeing her mother.

"Come here, baby," said Pearl.

Teflon walked toward her mother with the glass still in her hands. When Pearl saw the drink she questioned Teflon about it, taking the glass from her.

"Daddy made it for me. He says it's special, and he said he loves you too," Teflon childishly said.

"Oh he did, did he?"

"Um-hmm."

Pearl was convinced that Popsicle was tying to kill his own daughter. Hearing Teflon call him Daddy and telling her that he loved Pearl only confirmed how he got her daughter to trust him to consider drinking what he had made for her in the glass.

Pearl smelled the liquid and caught the whiff of the ammonia. Only God and Popsicle knew what else was in the mixture. Pearl and Popsicle stared at each other.

"Tef, go get your coat, baby. We leavin'," Pearl said as she stared at Popsicle.

Teflon ran and did as her mother said.

"Ho, you ain't goin' nowhere," shot Popsicle. Stepping in her direction, he pulled his .32 from behind his back. He pointed it toward Pearl's head. When he reached her, he grabbed her by the neck.

"Ho, you think you can just leave like that? I'll kill your funky ass first. You and that little bastard whore," shouted Popsicle as he cocked the hammer back on the pistol. Just as he did, Teflon came from out of the back room. Popsicle swung his gun in her direction. Believing that he was about to shoot her daughter, Pearl swung into combat mode. She spit out the razor she had in her mouth and caught Popsicle on the jugular, which caused Popsicle to swing his gun back on Pearl.

Reflexively, he let off two shots into Pearl's exposed midsection. Pearl instantly bellied over and fell to the floor. Popsicle then pressed his hand to his neck and began searching for something to compress the wound before he lost too much blood, as Teflon ran over to her mother.

"Mommy! Mommy!" she cried as she dropped to her knees. "Mommy, wake up!"

But Pearl did not move. The two bullets that riddled her body had killed her on impact, not even giving her time to realize what was taking place.

Seeing that her mother was not moving or listening to her, Teflon sat on the floor and lifted her mother's head as she placed it in her lap. Tears began to fall down her face as she stroked her mother's blond wig, rocking her back and forth the way Pearl use to do her. Out the corner of her eye, Teflon noticed Popsicle exiting the apartment with a towel pressed against his neck. Despite it being white, the towel was mostly red, Teflon noticed. That was the last time she had ever seen either of her parents again.

At age ten, Teflon was all alone, forced to turn to the streets. Games her mother had taught her and told her when she had been out with her on a few occasions while Pearl was out working invaded Teflon's mind. Games Pearl had shown her during the times when they were hungry and her mother's job wasn't going too well and Popsicle refused to feed them. "Go back there and get what you want while Mommy talks to the nice man at the counter, but make sure you hide it from me and show me later so it can be a surprise," Teflon remembered her mother whispering to her. "Here, open this, and let's see who can win by eating it the fastest. Ready—one, two, three, go!" was another game she recalled.

Teflon would have never imagined the game she disliked the most would later become a major asset to her as life progressed. "Tef, we're going to play a trick on that man over there. I want you to walk up to that nice white man and tell him you're lost and you need somewhere to sleep tonight." The first time, Teflon questioned her mother with tears in her eyes, thinking Pearl was abandoning her, but Pearl assured her she would never leave her. "Just trust Mommy, okay, precious?" Pearl answered, taking Teflon's face into the palms of her hands with tears filling her own eyes. Pearl hated having to use her pride and joy to fend for them in the streets. Although she wished things could be different for her little girl, she knew in her mind and felt in her heart that someday Teflon would have face what the streets consisted of. When that time came she wanted her to be ready.

"Excuse me, mister," Teflon would start out, gaining the trick's attention. Teflon did not understand why the man had been looking at her in the fashion he had when she first approached him. The look stemmed from the thought of bedding a young girl. It was the same look Teflon had noticed in every man's eyes that she and her mother had played the trick on.

"Yes, little lady, how may I help you?" they would all ask differently.

"I'm lost and have nowhere to go. Can I sleep at your house tonight?" Teflon would ask innocently. Pearl would stand watching from afar with anger and pain intertwining in her eyes while her stomach twisted in knots. God forbid someone snatched her daughter and she was unable to get a shot off with the .22 caliber she possessed.

"Why, sure you can, li'l darling," they would answer hesitantly as they looked around, making sure they were not being watched as they intended to do the unthinkable.

"Where's your mommy or daddy?" some of them would ask, but Pearl had prepared Teflon for the rebuttal. "I don't have one. Would you be my daddy?"

That often did the trick. "Yes, sweetheart, I'll take care of you. I'll be your daddy," was usually the response.

Just as the strangers warmed up to Teflon, Pearl would pop up and make a scene, threatening to call the police unless she was paid off with hush money. Sometimes things turned out differently and Pearl actually had to turn her con into a robbery. Teflon visited old areas that her mother frequented when they were out all night. Teflon remembered the many nights they had slept in some of the apartments that were boarded up with no traces of heat or electricity.

"Stay here, Mommy gotta go make some money," Pearl would tell her. And when the sun came up Teflon would wake to a bagel or breakfast sandwich. For the first two years on her own, Teflon went from one abandoned apartment to another. When she wasn't trying to catch a few hours of rest she was out trying to scrounge up her next meal. At age thirteen Teflon blossomed into an even prettier girl. She still possessed the clothes she had taken years prior, which belonged to her mother. She had grown right into the designer garments. By then Teflon had discovered what it was her mother actually did for a living. Though she still used the tricks and trades that were handed down to her by Pearl, Teflon was smart enough to know she wanted no parts of prostitution, but pretended to.

Teflon became extremely good at propositioning men who bought sex for money. She was now old enough and experienced enough in the streets to know the familiar look that all men possessed when they looked at her. Teflon had actually learned the true meaning when a trick tried to abduct her. Fortunately for her, she had inherited her mother's fast wit and instinct, not to mention her expertise with a razor. Teflon was able to break free of the would-be abductor by slicing the side of his face open like a cantaloupe, all in one motion and movement of the head. It was that incident that bettered her situation. As luck would have it, when she dug into the trick's pocket as he was on the ground screaming in agony, she retrieved a wad of cash consisting of twenty-five hundred crisp one-hundred dollar bills. But what Teflon didn't know at the time was that just as she had inherited her mother's hustling skills, she had also inherited her soft heart. It was the same heart that caused Teflon to find herself in the detention center after meeting Mike a year later. Mike, known as Blue Mike, was a tall, athletic built nineteen-year-old young hustler from Virginia Beach who was on the rise in the streets of Virginia.

His dark complexion and favorite color coined him the nickname Blue. At the time, Teflon had no interest or ties with the drug side of the streets, and he was a loner with no friends. She had never heard or seen the Morris Chestnut look-alike, not until that uneventful day they had literally ran into each other during Labor Day weekend on the strip of Virginia Beach.

The summer was coming to an end and Virginia Beach's main strip was flooded with bodies up and down the boulevard. Females young and old wore next to nothing with designer purses in hand and bags thrown over their shoulders, while guys over-accessorized with authentic and fake platinum and iced-out shines and rocked the latest designer gear. From Benzes to Beamers and Bentleys to Porsches and Aston Martins, everything cruised the strip, driven by young brothers who had some of the baddest black sisters in the country riding shotgun. This was the last major event of the summer before going back to school or in some cases back to the block of their respected hoods or wherever they conducted their illegal businesses. Those who attended were eager to make their visit to the beach area a memorable one. Brothers were looking for the best jump-off to add to their collection of stories of previous events, and the females were looking for that no-strings-attached fling or major come-up hoping to catch an out-of-state or in-town baller. Blue Mike was there for those same reasons. This was his third year attending, but this was his first coming correct.

Mike had first hit the Virginia Beach festival when he was sixteen. It was also the year and event that encouraged him to get in the game after seeing so many young brothers flossing and the females overlooking him, not giving him the time of day. The second year, Blue Mike hit the scene with his burgundy Acura Legend coupe sitting on three-star Antera rims. He had hustled all year to scrape up the cash to buy the whip and rims just for the Virginia Beach affair he remembered. Blue Mike had never been shown so much love from other hustlers and gotten so many numbers and one-night stands from so many fine women in his life as he did that three-day weekend. Blue Mike was among the elite in his home state, climbing the ladder in the drug trade, after he had robbed and allegedly murdered some Jamaican dealers from out of Brooklyn for 200 pounds of exotic weed and a 100-plus grand. He was stepping on the scene with his latest toy, a black Acura NSX. Blue Mike had fallen in love with Acuras. He liked the way they rode and how reliable they were.

At first, Blue Mike hadn't noticed the girl running toward his car until he began making a slow turn to the right. As she got closer, the look on her face told Blue Mike the girl was in distress. When he dropped his head low to lock in the miniature commotion, the three familiar faces trailing the girl confirmed his suspicion. Mike was a sucker for a pretty face, big butt, and smile, and the girl possessed all three. Just as the three angry-looking dudes caught up to the pretty girl, Blue Mike sprung into action.

"Yo, where you been?" he directed to the girl as he hopped outta the car. Recognizing Mike, the three young hustlers ceased pursuit.

Exhausted and out of gas, despite not knowing what he was talking about, the pretty girl was thankful he had aided her. She knew she had no more juice left in her legs after running for what seemed like an hour straight.

"Blue, she with you?" one of the hustlers asked in disbelief.

"Yeah. Didn't you know that?" Blue Mike shot back.

Passersby slowed to get an earful of the confrontation.

"Not me," one of the other hustlers quickly stated.

"Me neither, dawg," the third hustler said.

"What happened?" Mike was curious to know. Just as the three hustlers knew of Mike's reputation, he also knew of theirs. Mike knew the three were by far no cowards and were also known for putting in work. Fortunately for him, he had his Glock tucked in his lower back in case things took a turn for the worse.

"Nah, it wasn't about nothing," the first hustler answered. If this was Blue Mike's girl, there was no way he could tell him that he had pushed up on his girl, how they had been chilling together for the past few hours, how they had gone back to his room with the intentions of sexing, and how he had came out of the shower just in time to catch her emptying out his linen pants pockets and snatching up his jewels, which led to him calling up his boys and their taking pursuit.

"So why was you chasin' her?" Mike asked. He knew the hustler was lying and why, but Mike just wanted to know.

"It's mistaken identity. We thought she was someone else," the hustler continued to lie. In his mind, he had already chalked what the girl had stuck him for back at the hotel up as a loss. Besides, the jewels weren't real and there was only 110 dollars in his pockets. A small price to pay to prevent a war over a female, thought the hustler.

"It happens," Blue Mike remarked slyly. The girl let out a sigh of relief. "Yo, get in the car," he told her. She looked at him as if he were crazy. He shot her a look back that forced her to weigh her options. The three hustlers watched as the pretty girl opened Blue Mike's car door and got in. Now convinced she was in fact with him, the hustlers all dispersed and faded into the crowd.

"So what was that all about?"

"Nothing," she answered nonchalantly.

"Okay, if that's how you want it, but I don't get no thanks or nothing?"

"Look, if that's what this is about, you can pull over right here. I ain't no trick, and I can handle myself," she snapped.

"Whoa, whoa, I ain't the enemy, baby." Mike laughed. "It's cool. You want me to pull over, I will, but I wasn't tryin'a say you owe me nothing. I did what I did because that's just me. I wouldn't feel right lettin' you out right here knowing them dudes might spot you again and put two and two together. Just tell me where you wanna go and I'll drop you off, no strings attached."

Mike was turned on by the pretty girl's feistiness. Though he would comply with any request, he really didn't want her to leave his side. She was glad Mike had clarified things. She found him to be very attractive and would've hated to spit her blade out and distort his handsome face, though she had no problems doing so.

"So where to?"

"I'm hungry," she said.

"Not a problem." Mike couldn't believe his luck. He hadn't been on the strip ten minutes and already had bagged who he thought to be the baddest female out there.

"You got a name?"

She contemplated what name she would give. She had so many to choose from. That was something she had adopted from her mother. "Teflon."

Mike stared at her for a minute. "Are you serious?"

"Yeah. You got a problem with my name?" she snapped.

"Nah, baby, that's some fly shit. I thought you just made it up."

Teflon smiled for the first time since he had come to her rescue.

"You got a name?" she mocked him.

"Yeah, it's Mike. People call me Blue Mike, though."

"I wonder why," Teflon joked.

"Yeah, me too."

Teflon and Mike spent the remainder of the day together. After that, the two were nearly inseparable. Teflon never told Mike what she was into prior to their meeting or what took place that day on the strip and Mike never asked. Had he known, it might have made a difference. For the first time in her life, Teflon was really happy. Mike saw to it that she wanted for nothing. Not used to having anyway, there was not too much Teflon wanted in the first place besides the love of Mike. She was really thankful for the fact that she no longer had to live the type of life she had been before she and Mike had met. In him, she had a boyfriend and father figure all wrapped in one and that was fine by her. She didn't care what he did outside of their household, because at the end of the day he always found his way back in and took care of home base.

Being a hustler's wifey definitely had its perks, thought Teflon, and she was content with her position. But the flip side of the game never dawned on her until the day she and Mike came home from their favorite restaurant. Now Teflon sat in the detention center on room lock with hatred and resentment toward Blue Mike and all other hustlers. Teflon vowed to never get involved with a drug dealer ever again and told herself it was better to stick to what she knew best. She couldn't wait for the next sixteen months to go by.

Chapter Twelve

Teflon's forty-five days of room restriction had ended. Being in the room for so long and just eating and resting, she had put on a few pounds, filling out her 112-pound frame into an even 120 pounds, all eight pounds going into the right places. Her hair had also grown at least two-and-a-half inches from keeping it in two, but today she wore it all pulled back in one big ponytail, which showed off her cornrows of good hair. Teflon had actually enjoyed her little room vacation. It gave her time to gather her thoughts, but now that she had gotten them together she wanted to be allowed to interact with the others, one person in particular.

Treacherous scratched the day's date off his calendar as soon as he woke. He had been counting down the forty-five days they had given the new girl, and now those days were up. Throughout that time he had done less reading and more working out, trying to get better toned. He had always had a nice chiseled physique, but it was something about Teflon that caused him to want to work out harder. He went from doing a thousand push-ups a day to doing fifteen hundred, along with increasing his crunches from 750 a day to a thousand, adding to his washboard stomach. When he had weighed himself two days before, he had gone up from 170 pounds to 182 pounds solid with only 10 percent body fat. Treacherous was impressed with the twelve pounds in forty-five days of bulk he had put on. Dropping down, doing 120 push-

ups in one set, Treacherous was ready to hit the chow
hall, anticipating it being a good day.

The staff was a little leery about allowing Teflon to
return to general population, especially not knowing how
Treacherous would react to seeing the girl again, so they
decided to monitor both of their behavior and would be
alert for anything. The last thing they wanted to see was
Treacherous half killing the little feisty young girl.

All the other inmates had been doing their own counting down to Teflon's release, placing bets on how long it
would take for her to go back into lockup or get strangled
by Treacherous, betting their breakfast, lunch, and dinner trays. The detention center had gotten live in the past
month and a half. Some kids from Norfolk had gotten
arrested in a drug raid and smuggled some weed inside,
and six new girls, three who were young prostitutes, had
came up in there, so everybody was trying to get in on the
action. The kids who had possession of the weed had both
heard about and respected Treacherous, so they offered
him a nice chunk, figuring he either smoked or wanted to
trick with the young prostitutes, who were giving other
inmates hand jobs and blow jobs for food and weed.
Some of the inmates were even taking chances, sliding
up in the bathroom or one of the classrooms with them
unnoticed, sexing the young prostitutes. But Treacherous
wasn't concerned with any of that. He didn't get high nor
did he trick. He did take the weed, though, and stash it in
a book he knew nobody would touch because none of the
kids up in there really read books.

All the girls were attracted to Treacherous, and tried to
entice him in hopes of becoming his jailhouse girlfriend
by flashing their breasts at him and propositioning him,
but he was only interested in one girl. Treacherous sat at
his regular table by himself as he saw the young girls lined
up, coming from off the female side. In total, including

Teflon, there were now eleven girls, which was the most Treacherous had ever seen in the juvenile facility at one time the whole four years and some change he had been there.

For a minute Treacherous thought Teflon had not been a part of the female lineup, and wondered where she was, but right before the door had fully closed, Treacherous saw her.

Teflon came through with that same style and grace Treacherous remembered from the first time he laid eyes on her, still looking as if she didn't belong in such a place. As she entered the dining area, their eyes met just like before.

Treacherous tried to play it off and act as if it were just coincidence that he happened to look in her direction, but he couldn't help but to notice how good those forty-five days were to her. He could see she had blossomed into something even more beautiful while in isolation, seeing that she had put on a few pounds in all the right places and her hair had even grown. One of the girls had noticed the inconspicuous way Treacherous was looking at Teflon. "Girl, that nigga checkin' you out," the girl volunteered.

"Mind your fucking business," Teflon swung around and snapped, irritated by the girl's nosiness. The girl started to snap back with a sly remark but thought better of it. Teflon continued to watch Treacherous as he glided to his usual spot. Her heart skipped a beat. Treacherous sat there at the very same table he had been sitting at the first time she had ever seen him, only this time he was much bigger. He could have easily passed for a Greek god or a poster child for a muscle magazine, she thought, seeing the indentions of his physique through his shirt as his trap muscles sat up just below his ears.

Although they didn't realize it at the time, all eyes were on them. Everyone wanted to see the outcome of Treacherous and Teflon's reunion. Some kids snickered under their breaths, anticipating the worse, while others who bet in favor of Treacherous humbling himself thought the opposite. Staff was just ready for whatever way it went. It was their job to secure the safety of the institution and that was their only concern.

Teflon got her breakfast and began looking around as if she was in search of a seat, but it was only to buy her some time to get her thoughts together and decide whether she really wanted to go through with her intentions, because she already knew where she intended to eat. One of the guys who tried to push up on her when she first arrived motioned for her to sit with him and his clown friends, but Teflon acted as if she hadn't seen him. She made up her mind and walked toward her intended destination.

Treacherous observed Teflon looking around for what he assumed to be a place to sit. He started to motion for her to come and chill with him, but thought better of it, because he knew that wasn't gangsta, but when he saw the punk kid to his right, Fats, try to get her to come chill with him and his boys, Treacherous's blood began to boil. At the sight of Teflon ignoring them and heading toward him, he began to calm down, but had she accepted the punk kid's invitation, Treacherous knew he would've gone over there and punched the kid in the face just on general principle. As childish as it may have seemed, that's just how Treacherous got down.

Fats was positive Teflon had seen him trying to get her attention and she deliberately ignored him. Had he not seen her walking toward Treacherous he would have screamed on her and embarrassed her in front of everybody, but unbeknown to him, not going with his first instinct saved him from a crucial beat down, because he was not aware of what was taking place between Treacherous and Teflon, and could not have known that had he disrespected Teflon like the way he initially started to, Treacherous would've pounded on him the way a hammer does a nail.

Everybody watched as Teflon stopped in front of Treacherous's table.

"Can I sit here?" she asked with confidence.

"Go ahead, it ain't mine," replied Treacherous nonchalantly.

Hearing Treacherous's voice did something to her. The baritone sound made her want to surrender to him in every way possible but she maintained her composure as she sat down. Treach had waited forty-five days for this day and now that it had arrived he wasn't too sure how he wanted to handle it. He was not use to talking to females, so he didn't really know what to say. The only thing he could strike up a conversation about was jail things, but he didn't want to discuss that because he was living it, so why talk about it. He wondered if he should start with an apology, but quickly erased the thought because he didn't owe her one when he didn't do anything to her. The thought of everyone staring at him caused him to clench his teeth. He didn't have to look around to know that they were. He could feel their eyes all on the side of his face and continued to eat his breakfast, thinking of where to begin.

Teflon had thought about what she would say to Treacherous the whole forty-five days she was on room restriction. She had rehearsed her opening over and over until it sounded right to her, but as she sat before him, all she had rehearsed faded out of her mind, and her thoughts became a blur. She noticed all the other girls were staring at her like she was crazy, and she rolled her eyes at them. You would've thought she and Treacherous were playing the leading role in a drama movie the way everyone was focused on them. Teflon knew even if Treach wanted to say something to her first, he wouldn't because his reputation was on the line, so she knew she would have to be the one to take the iniative. Teflon took a deep breath and then exhaled.

"Um, Treach."

Hearing the soft-toned voice speak his name caused Treacherous to stop eating and look up. He had no idea Teflon possessed such a beautiful, smooth voice. On the last encounter she had she sounded just as rough—if not rougher—than the average dude in there when she stood up to him, he thought.

Teflon knew she now had his attention hearing her say his name, so she continued.

"I want to apologize for what I'm—"

"You don't owe me any apology," Treacherous interrupted. "That shit wasn't about—"

She cut him off. "Yes, it was about something. I had no right flippin' out on you like that that day. I ain't even—"

"Hold on," Treacherous interrupted again. "Yo, mind your mutha'fuckin' business," he barked to all who had been paying close attention to him and Teflon, some even leaning out of their seats. Everyone began to act as if they were involved in something other than Treacherous and Teflon's conversation.

Teflon smiled on the inside at how Treacherous had checked the whole dayroom. Even the staff began to mind their business after hearing the power and strength behind Treacherous's words. It was apparent that rather than a problem, there was a connection between the two inmates.

"My bad, pardon me. What were you sayin'?"

Teflon continued. "I was just sayin' I ain't even know you like that to be screamin' on you the way I did, and it was my bad. I know you got a lot of time up in here and a lot of respect, more than I ever seen one person have, and I wanted you to know I didn't mean to disrespect you because like everybody else, I respect you too."

Treacherous looked Teflon in her eyes as she spoke, and she never broke her stare. Even most of the dudes he had come across who professed to be thorough could not hold a stare as long as Teflon had when she spoke. Treacherous knew she was not like any other female he had ever known. Most girls always showed a sign of weakness or vulnerability, but even in her apology Treacherous detected nothing but strength and security. He was intrigued to know more about this beautiful gangstress.

"Yo, I respect you for respecting me enough to get at me like this, but that shit we went through is over just like the forty-five days you just did. I could've handled the situation differently too, but it is what it is, you know what I'm sayin'? We cool, ain't no beef, and if you have any problems while you up in here let me know; I don't care if it's inmates or staff, I got your back," Treacherous stated firmly.

"And I got yours too," Teflon replied.

Treacherous looked at her awkwardly, then shot her a half smile that only she caught.

"A'ight, I respect that."

Teflon shot him the same half grin. She had never blushed before the way she was blushing at that very moment.

"A'ight, shorty, I'll catch you later. You cuttin' into my reading time," said Treacherous, getting up from the table.

Teflon did not want him to leave, but she understood he had a set schedule. Before she left up out of there she intended to become a part of his daily schedule as well. It dawned on her they hadn't been properly introduced.

"Wait," she called out as Treacherous began walking away.

"What up?"

"You don't even know my name," she said.

"Yes, I do. Miss Teflon Jackson," Treacherous replied before walking away, but that would be the last time he would ever walk away from her again because from that day forward Treacherous and Teflon were inseparable.

Six months later things between Treacherous and Teflon had strengthened beyond anyone's imagination, and no one but Treacherous and Teflon themselves liked it. Other male inmates hated and despised Treacherous from afar because they wanted to be him while they lusted over Teflon. The female inmates who once thought they had a chance with Treacherous felt the same about Teflon. Every so often, a new girl was gassed up or one of the regulars built up enough heart and nerve to step to Treacherous, only to feel the wrath of Teflon, who didn't play when it came to Treacherous. Before her sentence at the detention center was complete, she had received room restriction three separate occasions, badly injuring three girls who tried to move in on her man. Staff thought Teflon to be a bad influence on Treacherous. Often they tried to separate the two, to no avail. They even went as far as trying to get Treacherous transferred to the county jail but never had good reason to because he never gave them one. Ever since Teflon had came into the picture Treacherous had been reserved and humble. He tried to keep Teflon at bay but couldn't control her temper when it came to her jealousy. Treacherous assured her that he only had eyes for her. To prove it, with the metal part of a number two pencil he carved a set of eyes in his arm with her name overtop.

Although she believed Treacherous's every word, Teflon didn't trust other females. Her motto was what was hers was hers and Treacherous belonged to her. Treacherous went through hell every time Teflon was locked down. He enjoyed her company and conversation and missed it whenever she got into trouble. They would talk about what they were going to do together when they were both released. The days couldn't go by quicker enough for Treacherous, but they were steadily approaching, he knew. Teflon would be released first but Treacherous knew he wouldn't be too far behind.

Teflon was on room lock once again and though he missed her, Treacherous was also heated with her. He tried to defuse the situation that caused Teflon to be confined to her room, but she wouldn't listen, and now after her room lock was over, in sixty days she would be going home and Treacherous knew he wouldn't see her again until his release. Treacherous shook his head in disappointment as he played the tape back that lead to Teflon's predicament.

"Hey, Treach," Carmen chimed, approaching the table where Treacherous played solitaire. Carmen was the newest female in the detention center. She was an attractive Hispanic sixteen-year-old from Richmond but was caught shoplifting in Military Circle Mall.

"What do you want, Carmen?" Treacherous asked, not bothering to look up. He knew Carmen liked him, but he paid her no mind. Not that Carmen made it easy for him. She was a nice sight on the eyes and she knew it. She stood five feet nine with still room to grow. Her hair was black with blond highlights, which matched her smooth skin tone. Both her body and facial features favored Jennifer Lopez. Often Treacherous would have to turn away from Carmen. She would flash one of her 34Cs at him whenever Teflon wasn't in sight. Once, Treacherous noticed Carmen fondling herself, while licking her lips, which always seemed as if they were laced with MAC lip gloss. Even if he weren't with Teflon, Treacherous knew he was not attracted to Carmen's demeanor. She was sexy as hell, but behaved like a common ho.

"You," she boldly answered.

"Get out of here, Carmen, 'fore you get yourself into something you can't get out of," Treacherous remarked drily.

"I know you don't think somebody scared of that chick. Maybe these other *puntas* is but not me, sweetheart, I'm Boriqua, and I ain't from around here. I'm from Richmond, the projects, baby!" Carmen announced.

Right at that moment, Teflon was returning from the restroom. Instantly she zeroed in on Carmen hovering over Treacherous. Her blood began to boil. She remembered what Treacherous had said about her temper and tried to calm herself. She wanted to spend her remaining two months left with him before she was released. Everyone watched as Teflon made her way over to Carmen and Treacherous.

"Yeah, *papi,* I bet you never had your dick sucked the way I could suck it. And I bet'cha I could find out how many licks it takes—"

That was all Teflon had to hear to make her spring into action.

Carmen being Hispanic made it convenient for Teflon to grab a fistful of her long silky hair. Carmen never saw it coming. Teflon flung Carmen around so rapid and forcefully that she got whiplash. "Ugh," she bellowed as she hit the floor. Teflon immediately pounced on top of her. She intended to make an example out of her as she commenced to pounding on Carmen's beautiful pecan face. She wanted all the other females in the detention center to see what they'd be facing when they got released if she heard they tried to move in on Treacherous while she was gone. By the time the slaughter was over, both of Teflon's hands were swollen from the beating she had put on Carmen while both of Carmen's eyes were purple, she had swallowed two teeth, and was treated for a fractured collarbone from the fall.

The day Teflon was released one of the girls Teflon knew was trustworthy delivered a letter from her to Treacherous, who upon receiving it immediately went to his room and locked himself in. The letter was folded as small as it could be, taped on all four corners. Treacherous smiled as he fought to unwrap the missive she had tried so hard to secure. Whenever Teflon would receive room lock, she and Treacherous would write each other and send their letters to one another through the same girl. Each time he opened one of Teflon's notes it always started out the same.

For your eyes only. That was one of the things he admired and had grown to love about Teflon. Treacherous finally opened up what would be his last letter from Teflon. He had told her specifically not to write when she got out. She was disappointed until Treacherous explained how once they were released there was no looking back. Confinement would be a thing of the past. The next time they would see or hear from each other they would both be free of bondage. Treacherous lay back on his bunk and opened the yellow-lined paper.

For your eyes only!

Hey baby,

I know you're probably still mad at me, but don't be. You know how I am when it comes to you. I told you before, I tried to keep my cool like you always tell me to, but I couldn't let that one slide. That was just total disrespect. That chick had it coming to her anyway. I think I did good, cause, I never said anything but I knew she used to be flashing you and playing with herself when I wasn't around. Yeah, you didn't think I knew that. Our mail carrier used to tell me. I had her watching you. She told me you used to be turning your head, lucky for you (smile). But when I heard her talking about putting you in her mouth and all of that, that was it, she had to get it. Besides, I'm the only one who's going to be doing that. Yeah, I said it. I can't wait until you come up out of that hellhole. I remember everything we talked about, but by the time you get here I will have already gotten a few things established for us. I know you told me don't worry about that other thing, but baby, trust me, I got it. That muthafucka owe and he gonna pay, one way or another. I don't have to tell you to hold your head in there because you were doing that before we met, I think that's what attracted me to you; in fact, I know. Those eighteen months being in there with you were the best months of my life, and I wouldn't change them for nothing. I hope you feel the same. You better, nigga (smile). So, this is it, our last letter. Baby, it's been real, and it's gonna get even realer when you hit the bricks. Until then . . . Love you!

'Til Death Do Us Part,
Your Ride Or Die Chick

Like always, Treacherous grinned at the end of Teflon's note. She always made it her business to let Treacherous know she was with him no matter what, to the bitter end, even when he told her his plans once released. Treacherous shredded the note and tossed it in the toilet. All he could think about was the six months he had remaining.

Chapter Thirteen

Six months later . . .

Teflon sat outside the detention center, straddled across her Yamaha R1 motorcycle with her customized helmet in hand waiting impatiently for Treacherous. The past six months had been torture for her being away from him. When she was first released it had been a struggle for her coming home. She and Treacherous had discussed her taking advantage of the little housing room the state had offered her upon her release, providing she found a job and laying low until he came home, then together they would get all they needed. That was the plan, but Teflon grew impatient. Besides, there was no way she was going to let her man come home to nothing. Teflon had no regrets going out and making something happen so that Treacherous had everything he would need once he was released. Nor did she have any remorse for the hustlers who she baited and lured in to obtain the money that had taken care of her for the past six months and allowed her to get what she felt Treacherous needed. Treacherous meant more to her then anything else in the world. Teflon had schemed on and robbed six above-average hustlers, one for every month, coming off with a little over 70,000 in cash and jewelry. It seemed like an eternity since the last time she had seen or heard from Treacherous, but as she looked at her Cartier watch, she knew in mere minutes all of that would be coming to an end. Every time the tinted glass door to the front entrance opened her heart skipped a beat, hoping it was Treacherous who was exiting. It was a few minutes after Treacherous's 9:00 a.m. release. Each minute that passed, Teflon grew more and more impatient. By 9:30 Treacherous still had not come out.

"What the fuck?" Teflon sighed as 9:00 turned into 10:00. At 10:30, Teflon's patience wore thin. She couldn't take it anymore. She knew it was too good to be true. All types of thoughts began to invade her mind. She wondered if Treacherous had gotten himself into something. She didn't want to believe it but knew that anything was possible. Whatever the case, Teflon intended to find out. She un-straddled the R1 and made her way to the detention's center front door. Just as she reached the top of the steps the door was opening up. Teflon grabbed hold of the handle and stepped to the side to let whoever it was out.

"Thanks," the familiar baritone said.

Teflon was so caught up in her own world, focused on demanding answers and giving someone problems until they let her know what was going on with Treacherous, that she hadn't even noticed him coming out of the door.

"Baby!" she chimed, wrapping her arms around his neck.

Treacherous smiled on the surface, but on the inside he felt funny. He was not used to this type of affection.

"Yeah, it's me."

Teflon was tempted to break out into tears but she knew how Treacherous felt about that. He had shared with her how he had been raised and she understood. Teflon released Treacherous, sensing his discomfort. "What took so long?" she asked.

"Paperwork, not to mention the long speech the counselor gave me. Broad beat me in the head about nothing, all that whole-life-ahead-of-me bullshit."

"Same stuff they said to me before I left. Who was it, Ms. Brown?"

"Yep."

"Figured."

"You know what else she said?" Treacherous asked with a strange smirk plastered across his face.

"What?"

"She asked me to promise her to stay away from you. She said if I saw you to turn the other way."

"Stop playing," Teflon said with a surprised look.

"If I'm lying I'm dying."

"Fucking bitch," Teflon barked. "If her ass sees *me* she better turn the other way."

That caused Treacherous to laugh. "A'ight, killa, let's get up outta here," he said, grabbing her by the head. Teflon pulled away as if she were still bothered by the counselor's words. Treacherous could see how what he'd told her had affected her. "Tef, fuck that broad," he shouted, assuring her that what the counselor suggested didn't faze him.

Now it was Teflon who smiled as she made her way to the motorcycle.

"Whose is this?" Treacherous asked when Teflon walked up on the R1. He never noticed the helmet in her hand.

"It's mine."

"Yours?"

"Yeah, mine." Teflon knew he would be surprised. Especially since she had told him she didn't know anything about bikes, let alone ride when he expressed his passion for motorcycles. It was because of Treacherous that Teflon had gone out and brought one and learned how to ride.

"I thought you didn't ride."

"That was then." She grinned. "This is now. You inspired me."

"Oh yeah. Well, where's mine?" he joked.

"At our place," she replied.

Treacherous stared at Teflon oddly, as if she spoke a language foreign to him.

"What?"

"You asked where was yours and I said at our place," she repeated.

"Yeah, a'ight," said Treacherous, playing along with Teflon. "What you get me?"

"A GXSR 1000."

Something in the way Teflon had called out the bike made Treacherous feel she was not playing with him.

"Baby, you for real?"

"As a heart attack."

Treacherous's face remained emotionless but internally he was overwhelmed. At that moment he realized Teflon was indeed his ride or die chick.

"Let's get up outta here. Take me home so I can see my shit."

"You drive," Teflon said, tossing Treacherous the keys.

The R1 barked as he revved the engine. Teflon grabbed hold of his waist as Treacherous popped the clutch into first gear. He had never ridden before, only remembered what his father had told him, but just sitting on the powerful machine made Treacherous feel as if he had been riding all of his life. Just as Rich had explained to him, Treacherous slowly released the clutch. Once in first gear, he gassed up her bike. The tires screeched as he pulled off. Teflon looked back and stuck her middle finger up at the detention center, then tightly grabbed hold of Treacherous's waist as they headed home.

"Baby, you'll have plenty of time to ride. It ain't going nowhere," Teflon called out to Treacherous. When they arrived at the Yorkshire apartment complex Teflon had been staying in for the past six months, Treacherous zeroed in on the motorcycle parked out front. On sight, he fell in love with the machine. He had been home for nearly an hour and hadn't made it inside their apartment yet, overwhelmed with the bike. He was like a kid with a new toy. Treacherous had been so caught up in the bike he hadn't heard anything Teflon had said.

"Treach, did you hear me?" she shouted, walking toward him.

"Huh?" Treacherous answered, turning toward Teflon. Instantly he noticed her attire. "You tryin'a make me catch a body first day home, huh?"

Teflon laughed. "What?" she asked innocently. She became so impatient with Treacherous she hadn't realized she had just stepped out of the apartment with a pair of boy shorts that did nothing to conceal her God-given assets. The shorts rode up between her inner thighs and the cuff of her firm ass hung slightly out in the back. The fitted wife beater minus the bra didn't help the situation either. This was actually the first time Treacherous had ever seen so much of Teflon exposed, although he had a strong idea it existed. He liked what he saw and was instantly turned on.

"Go in the house," he said, not wanting anyone to see what he felt was for his eyes only.

"You come in the house too," Teflon replied seductively. "You acting like you love that bike more then me. Don't make me blow that shit up," she spat, her demeanor and tone changing from soft to aggressive.

"You the only one I want, babe," Treacherous stated. "The only one. I'm coming; now go inside."

"Get off the bike," she chimed. Treacherous knew he was fighting a losing battle. He was used to Teflon acting the way she was now. He hopped off the bike and made his way toward her. "What am I gonna do with you?" he said, grabbing Teflon from behind, wrapping his arms around her.

"Everything," she answered.

***

"Thanks for the meal, babe," Treacherous said to Teflon, reaching over to give her a kiss.

"You know you don't have to thank me. You're my heart. I just wanted everything to be nice for you," she replied, embracing him. "You're home now. This is just the beginning." She continued to wash the upper part of Treacherous's back. He relaxed in the bath she had prepared for him. He had been soaking for half an hour while Teflon bathed him. She knew this was what he had needed, just coming home. After serving eighteen months herself, it was what she had needed to convince herself that she was really home. Teflon dipped the washcloth into the water, then squeezed it out over top of Treacherous's clean-shaven head. His dome glistened as the suds washed away. Teflon massaged his pecs as she continued to wash the residue off him, causing it to cascade from his head onto his chocolate chest, which was rock solid. Each part of his body she touched was hard and chiseled with muscles. That turned Teflon on. This was the first time she had ever seen the results of Treacherous working out in the detention center religiously.

"This shit feels good. I couldn't wait to get up outta there and get that jail funk off me. Babe, I ain't never going back. We ain't never going back, you hear me" he spat in disgust, turning toward her.

"I know, baby, I hear you," Teflon agreed. She could hear the hostility in Treacherous's tone. She knew he was bitter behind the years of his life that had been wasted in the detention center and knew there was nothing she could do to change that, but nonetheless, she intended to try. "Let's not dwell on that, Treach. Let's just focus on us and how we're going to get this money. Fuck all that other stuff. Remember: No looking back."

"Definitely, no looking back," he repeated. "Hand me a towel. I'm done." She reached over and retrieved the towel she had waiting for him. Treacherous stood and Teflon began to dry him. Treacherous's manhood grew as Teflon took him into her hand and began massaging it while drying him off. "Chill," Treacherous moaned, unable to bear her touch.

"You chill," she shot back. "Let me do this." Teflon knew that his body was foreign to her touch and sensitive from being without a woman's physical touch. Other then the time his father had treated him to the stripper, Teflon knew no other female had been this close to Treacherous and she felt special. Tonight she intended to make this a memorable one for both of them.

Teflon took Treacherous by the hand and helped him out of the bathtub. Treacherous revealed a half smile. He could tell Teflon had planned all that was taking place. Despite the inevitable once they were both free, this was something they had never discussed. Treacherous could hear the sound of R&B music coming from the bedroom as he followed Teflon. The closer they got, the more the sounds of Color Me Badd throwing back "I Wanna Sex You Up" could be heard. As Teflon glided down the hallway Treacherous's sex began to stiffen even more. The sight of her firmness from behind simultaneously and rhythmically bouncing from up underneath the wife beater she wore and her hips swaying from side to side was turning him on. Although he was not a heavy music listener, the sound of the music was appealing to him and fit the mood. When Teflon opened the bedroom door, the first thing Treacherous noticed was the king-size bed with satin sheets that were blue, his favorite color.

Teflon turned and kissed Treacherous lightly on his bare chest, then led him to the bed.

She sat at the edge of the bed and released the towel from around his waist. He made an attempt to move in closer but Teflon held him at bay, pressing her hands into his washboard midsection as he towered over her. Treacherous looked down at her. She could feel his eyes on her but didn't return his stare. Instead, without hesitation she took Treacherous into her mouth. Treacherous did not expect what was happening. The warmth of her mouth was indescribable. He had never felt the way he did at that very moment. Teflon gyrated her mouth back and forth on Treacherous's hardness. Having never performed fellatio before, she gagged a few times from the size of Treacherous's rock hardness. She could not even believe she was able to get so much as the head inside of her mouth, based on how Treacherous was packing. She grabbed hold of his waist for support. Even the side of his buttocks were sculpted and solid, she thought as she continued to sex Treacherous with her mouth.

Treacherous continued to enjoy Teflon's performance. He had never experienced such a feeling before. As strong as he felt himself to be, Treacherous couldn't help but grab hold of Teflon's shoulders for balance. Each time he felt Teflon's lips reach midway on his dick his legs nearly gave way under him. A few times he heard her choke as she tried to take him into her mouth deeper. He knew he was well endowed, but regardless of the size of his manhood, he was convinced that all the working out he had ever done had not conditioned him for the workout Teflon was putting on him. He watched as Teflon's head now smoothly began to bob back and forth on his ten inches of chocolate. He could hear Teflon slurping over the music as she popped his sex in and out of her mouth. Teflon's performance put him in the state of mind of a suction cup the way her lips locked around him. Slowly but surely she was getting the hang of oral as she was eager to learn every inch of Treacherous's body tonight. Although she could get into them, she had tried watching adult movies for pointers on how to please him and picked up on how to enhance the oral pleasure she was now displaying on him. He couldn't help but close his eyes and throw his head back, bracing himself with the help of her shoulders as she vigorously attacked his sex. The more Teflon licked, sucked, and jerked, the more the feeling became unbearable for Treacherous, who tried everything in his power to withstand the enjoyment brought to him by Teflon, but he knew he had to bring the pleasurable feeling to an end before he exploded.

Treacherous lifted his head back up and opened his eyes. When he looked down for a second time he saw she was staring up at him with him still in her mouth. Their eyes met. Fully turned on by the effect her mouth had on him, Teflon knew she was far from being a pro, still occasionally gagging and having to let up for air, but there was no doubt in her mind that Treacherous was enjoying every bit of it as she took all she could of him into her mouth. Treacherous couldn't help to look down and witness the love she was putting down on him. Their eyes met, and as she too stared up at him, she licked around his helmet. Neither of the two broke the stare. At that moment a connection was, one that only the two of them would ever know. Teflon ran her tongue down the spine of Treacherous's rock-hard shaft. The volume of his low moan increased at the feeling. She then took him back into her mouth, then out and licked her way down, reaching his nut sack. That was all he could bear. Treacherous pulled back and pushed Teflon's head off him. Teflon shot him a devilish grin. She could tell by the way his body slightly quivered that his sack was sensitive.

Teflon backed herself up onto the bed and parted her legs. "Come here," she called out to him, childlike with

a devilish grin plastered across her face as she extended
her hands out. Treacherous leaned in to her embrace. He
now had a clear view of Teflon's neatly shaven tunnel and
her smooth inner thighs. For the first time, he noticed
Teflon had a tribal tattoo on her waistline, which seemed
to wrap around. This was something Teflon had never
shared with him. Having a few himself, the ink work on
her turned Treacherous on. He placed one hand around
his dick. This was the hardest it had ever felt to him, he
thought. It was throbbing from the treatment it had just
received from Teflon.

She also reached out to Treacherous's manhood with
one hand while touching herself with the other. She was
on fire. Her love cave felt as if it were a volcano, dripping
with lava. Teflon grabbed hold of Treacherous. At that
moment all she wanted was to feel him inside of her. Only
he and he alone could cool her cave with his hose. "Come
here," she repeated. But Treacherous resisted. Instead,
he reached out and pulled her toward him. Treacherous
placed a light kiss on Teflon's forehead, then a hard one
to her lips. Teflon accepted the kiss as it turned into a
passionate one. The kiss seemed to last hours. It was
Treacherous who broke the lip lock. Treacherous was
now standing at the edge of the bed. He grabbed hold
of Teflon's wife beater and lifted it over her head as she
raised her arms. Teflon's vanilla-toned 36Cs bounced out
of the wife beater. Treacherous cupped them both and
put them together. He kneeled and began to nurse Teflon's pink left nipple, then did the same to the right. She
moaned. Chills shot through her body as Treacherous's
warm tongue tickled her nipples.

Treacherous took Teflon's left breast into his mouth.
While he squeezed her right mound with his left hand
and sucked the juice out it, he massaged Teflon's love
cave with the other. Treacherous felt her wetness. She

was dripping of her own sex. Her juices had overflowed onto Treacherous's hand. He could feel Teflon's hips rotating and grinding into his fingers. He heard her mumble through her moans but couldn't make it out over the sounds of the music dominating the air. Treacherous continued to travel downward, licking every inch and crevice of Teflon's body.

"Oooh," Teflon sighed, arching her back as Treacherous toyed with her navel with his tongue. Chills continued to jolt through her entire body from his touch. She had never been so turned on in her life. Treacherous made his way between Teflon's inner thighs, planting kisses and gentle bites between them. Never being between a woman's thighs before, Treacherous had no clue as to what he was doing, but he knew he wanted to reciprocate the love she had shown him.

Each time Treacherous pressed his teeth into Teflon's skin, she flinched. No one had ever gone down on her before, so she was sure that he was doing it right—because it was Treacherous, it felt right. She shifted her hips as she moaned from the pleasure the bites bought to her body. She began to enjoy the way he dug into her flesh with his mouth. It was more sensual than painful. Treacherous tried his best to please Teflon. Her scent drew him in and made him want to taste her. She had a natural scent, he thought. As the side of his face continued to brush up against and rest on Teflon's sex, he was ready to explore her in that way with his mouth. At age eighteen he was inexperienced sexually and knew nothing about oral sex. He knew that Teflon's body was responsive to him as his was to her, so the last thing he wanted was to dampen the mood by not being able to completely satisfy the woman he loved in the bedroom. But he knew the timing was right and it was now or never. Treacherous slowly turned his head to meet Teflon's sex. Her natural sweet-smelling fragrance between her legs as he was now full faced with her sex. He placed his mouth just below where Teflon should have possessed a patch of hair. He gently bit into her clit. "No," he heard her moan with her hands locked on the sides of his head. Teflon had been so caught up in Treacherous's lips and tongue on her body she hadn't noticed he had made his way to her pussy.

"What's wrong?" he asked, puzzled.

"Nothing, I just don't want you to. I wanna feel you inside me." Teflon knew when she had watched the porno tapes that she would not like oral sex performed on her. She knew she would be able to give but wasn't too thrilled about receiving. Though she never experienced sex before, she knew she would be more of a flesh-on-flesh type of sister. "Come here," Teflon said, pulling Treacherous toward her. Teflon's words shot straight to Treacherous's dick. His manhood stiffened more. He too would rather be inside Teflon than trying something he knew nothing about. Teflon parted her legs more and slid back onto the bed, then reached out and took hold of Treacherous's sex as he slid with her. Treacherous towered over her as Teflon tried to place the head of his hardness inside of her.

She sighed. When she first saw the size of his dick she knew it was going to be a problem. The only dick she had had before was Blue Mike's and he wasn't packing like Treacherous. It had also been awhile since she had taken dick.

"You okay?" Treacherous asked, concerned.

"Yeah, baby, I'm good," she said. "It's just that you're big and . . . Well, it's been a while, and it was only one person before you."

Her words caught Treacherous off guard. They had touched on many topics in the detention center, personal and in depth, and Teflon had never revealed her sexual past, even when he had disclosed his only sexual encounter. Although he was thrown, Treacherous was actually glad. It made him feel more at ease about his inexperience. He knew that after tonight he and Teflon would learn everything there was to know about each other sexually and that no one would touch the other ever again.

"Don't worry, I got you," Treacherous told her. He leaned in and began kissing Teflon slowly and passionately, taking hold of his manhood, rubbing it around Teflon's sex in a circular motion, then up and down, occasionally placing the head inside of her. Teflon continued to moan. She could feel herself getting even wetter from Treacherous's foreplay. She began kissing him harder, then gasped.

"I got you," Treacherous assured her, lifting up his upper body. Treacherous slid half of himself inside of Teflon. Her wetness allowed him to enter her with ease. The pain was excruciating for her, but pleasurable at the same time. She watched as Treacherous artistically got her sex to open up to him. Each time she tried to match his stroke her muscles tightened. The more Treacherous stroked, the wetter Teflon became. Treacherous's strokes became deeper. He could feel himself all the way inside of her now and so could she. Tears trickled down the side of her face from the foreign pain, but she refused to tell Treacherous to stop. It felt as if he were splitting her in two. Treacherous lay on Teflon as he continued pumping her insides. He could feel Teflon's juices all over him as her muscles clenched his. Treacherous cupped her butt cheeks and spread them apart. It felt as if he'd opened up a new door. Even Teflon felt the difference as she was now able to semi-match Treacherous's thrust. Treacherous slid his sex in and out of Teflon with ease. He could hear juices talking between the two of them. Treacherous felt he was ready to try a different position. Just when he was about to pull out and turn her over, Teflon wrapped her legs around him and locked him in.

"Oh shit, oh shit," she repeated. "Shit, baby, I'm about to cum." She thrust her hips into Treacherous. It was Treacherous who now had to match Teflon. "Ooh, yeah baby," she groaned.

That was all Treacherous could withstand. He felt himself building up inside. "Damn, damn," was all he could muster as he aggressively pumped his dick into Teflon. "Yeah, cum with me, baby," she cooed, digging her nails into his back.

"Agh, I'm cumin' babe, I'm cumin'" Treacherous growled, increasing his pace as Teflon's nails caused him to arch.

"Me too," Teflon announced, gyrating her hips into him. Together they battled for supremacy as their juices intertwined.

"That was good," an out-of-breath Teflon managed to say when they finished.

"Definitely," was what she got in return from an equally out-of-breath Treacherous.

Treacherous rolled off Teflon and onto the left side of the bed. Teflon leaned over and placed her head on Treacherous's rock-hard chest, throwing one of her legs over his. "I love you, Treach," she purred.

"I love you too, babe."

That night, Treacherous and Teflon made a connection that bonded them far beyond anyone's imagination.

Chapter Fourteen

Seven years later . . .

"Boo, you sure he holdin' like that?" asked Treacherous.

"Yeah, nigga, what I tell you? I been coming here for the past two months, and it's been the same thing every week. He comes in with his big-ass platinum chain with the iced-out Jesus piece on and iced-out platinum bracelet on one wrist and diamond bezel Cartier watch on the other, buying out the bar. It never fails. He pulls out about seven Gs out his pocket every week, so this week shouldn't be any different. And the nigga been tryin'a to get me to leave the club with him for the past two months, so I know I can get him up out of there," replied Teflon confidently.

Treacherous's veins tightened in his neck at the sound of hearing about the hustler pushing up on Teflon. Treacherous intended to make him pay for his flamboyance and thinking he could just push up on any chick 'cause he was making a couple of dollars, but he knew Teflon would have never fallen into that type of trap so many women did, because to her it was all just business. Her love and loyalty belonged strictly to Treacherous. They had been a team for the past seven years ever since they had been released from the youth house. Despite his request, Teflon had written to Treacherous every day for six months straight after she had gotten out, but Treacherous never wrote back. She knew in both her mind and heart he was coming home to her. As soon as Treacherous came home, he took Teflon's gun, went out, and robbed some jokers from the Tidewater projects. He chose that particular area, which was where he had grown up, because someone from up out of there cost him five-and-a-half years of his life in jail. The money he had gotten from them was enough to move Teflon up out of the apartment she had been staying in into a nicer one, and from that day forward Treacherous and Teflon had been on a rampage.

"Who that cat be with?" asked Treacherous.

"Nobody. He travels alone."

"Good, that's good. How long it's gonna take you?"

"Maybe about an hour, a little more."

"A'ight, go ahead and bring 'em up out of there, and be careful—you know some of them jokers be strapped up in there. If that cat got all that big shit on him, then you know he gotta have a big gun on him too."

"Boy, I got this. Just chill," Teflon replied as she walked toward the club.

Treacherous half grinned the way he always did when Teflon tried to check him. She was the only one who could get that off. He knew she was capable of handling herself in any situation because she had proven it time and time again, but Casablanca's was the hardest club in Norfolk since people could tote burners on them up in there, and dudes conducted business up in there so the majority of the heads were strapped. One particular time a known rapper came to perform and had to whip out his chrome .38 on another known gangster named Kenny Speed. He was not only rapping his rhymes, he was also rapping to Speed's chick and didn't know it. Just like he didn't know who Kenny Speed was and how close to death he had come, but Treacherous knew who he was and he knew who Treacherous was. They both had mutual respect for the other because they had both put in work on the same streets for the same cause, just as dudes like Little Lo, Stacey, Jay, Black Boo, Pablo, U-man, Kinyatta, Born, and other gangstas from up out of the Norfolk, Portsmouth, and Virginia Beach area did.

In the past Treacherous and Teflon had robbed both males and females coming up out of Mr. Magic's, David, and the Bridge, which was on the border of Norfolk and Virginia Beach, where Teflon caught her first shooting. Teflon recalled beefing with one of the girls from the Lex Coupe Chicks who was sweating Treacherous. Teflon was still very jealous and overprotective of Treacherous, even after he came home and stepped to the girl.

Sheraine, who owned the beauty salon Faces and was the head of the Lex Coupe Chicks, tried to intervene and dead the arising beef because she had heard of and knew Teflon by reputation and she knew her girlfriends weren't built like that to be popping shit to someone of Teflon's caliber, but before she could shut her girlfriend up, Teflon had already shot her in the leg and grazed her on the side of the face. After that night, no other woman dared to look at Treacherous as the word spread like wildfire how Teflon got down when it came to him. Treacherous and Teflon were known all throughout the area as a vicious duo, and robbery was their motive. They would ride their bikes, which they upgraded each year, to places like Military Circle Mall, MacArthur Center Mall, and Lynnhaven, where all the heavyweight money getters and mediocre ballers from up north went to shop. They would squat on them to come out, then jack them and speed off on the high-powered motorcycles. They even jacked hustlers who they saw car shopping on Virginia Beach Boulevard. They were so used to scoping people out they could tell when someone was actually holding a lot of money. Wherever hustlers dwelled, that's where you would find them. While others took the risk of makin' it, Treacherous and Teflon took the risk of taking it, which was much easier, they both thought, than dealing with all the headaches that came with the drug game. A few times Treacherous decided to jack a couple of cats he caught either coming up out of Kappatal Cuts or at the self-service on the corner of Brambleton and Park on his way to get a haircut, but laid off of them after the owner asked him to chill because it was bringing heat to the area, making it bad for business.

Treacherous never robbed anybody in the barbershop area again. He could recall times when some young hustlers would rebel after their friends warned them he and Teflon were coming. There was always one out of every bunch who had to prove to others he wasn't scared—or at least that's what he thought he was proving. When it was all said and done, the only thing he would have proved was that he was stupid enough not to tuck his jewelry or pass his paper off to a shorty and got yapped and occasionally bitch-slapped by Treacherous's pistol for taking too long to come up off his shit. Treacherous enjoyed the looks on people's faces as he and Teflon entered the parking lot of McDonald's off Princess Ann Boulevard. It was as though everyone was frozen in time, how still they would be. The only time Treacherous and Teflon turned down the heat in Norfolk was when there was some type of jam jumping off at Norfolk Scope. Whenever an event like that was going on, Treacherous's primary targets were strictly Portsmouth heads who had come across the water to get to Norfolk Scope with their hottest whips, flyest outfits, and most expensive shines, but the same way they drove into Norfolk was not the same way they drove out because Treacherous and Teflon made sure of that. Treacherous's motto was, "If you weren't from Norfolk then stay the fuck out of Norfolk."

Treacherous stood across the street from the Broadway, checking his watch, waiting for Teflon to lure their potential victim outside the club. He glanced at his watch he had taken off some young dealer and saw nearly two hours had gone by and still no sign of Teflon or the kid. After five more minutes of waiting, Treacherous noticed the front door of the club opening and stepping out the door was a tall, light-skinned guy who fit the description she had given, with Teflon hanging onto his arm. As he observed the two, he laughed on the inside, wondering who could resist Teflon with her Indian-textured hair pulled to the back, with no makeup, only the natural essence of her beauty, wearing a pair of Prada glasses, sporting a pink-and-white Baby Phat top, a pair of Apple Bottom capris, pink-and-white Air Force 1's, looking both sexy and gangsta. As Treacherous saw Teflon and the kid walking toward what he believed to be a 4.6 Range Rover, he pulled out his two desert eagles and started quickly walking in their direction.

Teflon was glad to finally be up out of the crowded club. It had taken her almost two hours of listening to the tall, lame kid. She couldn't wait to off the kid, who she thought too into himself. Teflon couldn't stand conceited people. All he had talked about was how he knew how to care of and please a woman like her inside and outside of the bedroom, practically telling her the size of his bankroll and what he had in his pants. Teflon didn't know whether it was all of the bubbly he had consumed or whether he just was naturally like that, but either way she was convinced he had a big mouth, something that had made him an eligible candidate for her intentions. On a few occasions he had pressed up against her while at the bar in an attempt to feel how turned on she had him—or he claimed she did—but not only did she feel the bulge down his pants, she also felt the bulge in his waistband too. Treacherous was right. He did carry a big gun, she thought. She made a mental note to disarm him once they got outside. Seeing that he had enough to drink, Teflon whispered in his ear she was ready to get up out of there and hit their little one-on-one after party. Hearing that, the kid was ready to bring his night to an end, imagining all the things he intended to do to this fine piece of ass he was fortunate enough to snatch up for the night.

Both Teflon and the kid exited the club together as all the other ballers watched. Had he been somebody they knew or had love for, they would have pulled his coat to what he was getting himself into. He was from New York, and in their opinion was down in the dirty, messing up the game with his cutthroat prices and elaborate spending on the local chicks, causing the price of pussy to go up. They felt the out-of-towner deserved whatever he was about to get. Everybody in the club but him knew Teflon was Treacherous's girl, so if she was up in the club they were sure Treacherous was not too far behind, possibly outside waiting for the stupid New Yorker.

"So, ma, what's really hood?" the guy asked her with a smile as he hit the alarm to his Range Rover, unlocking the SUV's doors. "I'm saying, I wasn't frontin' when I said I'm tryin'a see you for something if you ain't got no manz like you say."

"I told you. I'm single, boo. My man just caught thirty in the feds and ain't leave me with nothing," Teflon replied innocently, stepping toward the Range.

"Say no more, ma. I got you. You fuckin' with a real G now. You gonna be—" The out-of-towner was just about to finish his words when something caught his attention. Out the corner of his left eye he saw movement and he reached for the .357 long nose he had tucked in his waistband.

"Mu'fucka, you know what it is?" threatened Treacherous with a murderous tone, smacking the New Yorker with the .45 he possessed in his right hand, sending him to the ground and landing on one knee.

"Get ya bitch ass up," barked Treacherous, grabbing the guy by his multicolored Coogi sweater while he still had the gun in one hand. As Treacherous roughly assisted the New Yorker getting back up, Teflon had her ratchet out and pressed up against the back of the kid's head.

"Muthafucka!" the New Yorker yelled.

"Yeah, bitch, you got played!" shot back Teflon, mushing the kid in the head with his own gun, knowing he had just realized he had been set up.

"Fuck all that. Let me get that big-ass chain. Boo, hit that clown pockets, and take that muthafuckin' bracelet and watch off too, before I put something hot up in your ass," Treacherous boomed, wanting to get the stickup over and done with.

He stared into Treacherous's face intensely.

"Yeah, chump, go 'head and look," said Treacherous sarcastically, knowing the kid was recording Treacherous's appearance in his memory for future reference. "'Cause if you ever see this face ever again, it'll be the last face you see ever again."

Hearing that, the kid broke his stare before he pressed his luck. Teflon pulled out the two knots of money the kid had in each pocket and shoved them down her shirt. Treacherous knew it was time to break out, but he could not let it just end like that. He had to leave the kid something to remember him by, and take something from him more valuable than his shines.

"Mu'fucka, give me the keys," demanded Treacherous. The look on the kid's face was indescribable. Now that Treacherous was taking something from the kid he would always remember, it was now time to give him something before he and Teflon rolled out. He reached behind his back and pulled out a .38 special similar to the one his father used to tote and fired.

The kid went down in the blink of an eye. Treacherous had shot him in both of his kneecaps.

"You ever see me again, you better hop the other way, pussy!" shouted Treacherous as he jumped in the Range Rover and sped off. Teflon jumped on the Ducati and followed. Hearing the shots caused some of the partygoers who were coming up out of the Broadway to scatter, but those who were strapped instantly pulled out, ready for whatever. As the Range Rover jetted passed the crowd, everyone noticed the New Yorker in the street holding both legs and knew what happened. The kid shouted for someone to help, but no one did because to them he was an outsider, and regardless of how Treacherous and Teflon got down, they were family of Virginia.

Treacherous drove the stolen Rover if it were his own, not worrying about the police. He didn't mind abandoning the other car they drove up to the club because it too was stolen, not to mention it was a hooptie. Teflon trailed close behind him, carefree. What took place was nothing new to her. She had seen Treacherous handle situations far worse than back at the club. To her, the kid made out lucky. He had only suffered knee injuries and temporarily lost the functioning of his legs. Others weren't so lucky— they had lost their lives. However Treacherous chose to handle a situation was fine by her. No matter what, she had his back and she was sure that he had hers.

"Wait right here," Treacherous told Teflon as they reached a secluded area and stopped. Teflon asked no questions. She already knew what he was about to do.

Treacherous pulled within a hundred yards of a brick wall and threw the Range in park. He then hopped out and began looking around. He retrieved a medium-sized stick, put it between the seat and gas pedal, put the Range in drive, and let it take its course. Teflon sat on the Ducati and watched as the Range Rover smashed into the brick wall. To her and Treacherous, the truck was worthless. Neither of them were into materialistic things. They did not care about the things in which average black people who ran and indulged in the streets cared about, like cars, jewelry, and clothes or who was doing what, when, and how. Although they lived in a material world, material things did not define them. Their only concern in the streets was money and lots of it, so whatever it took to get it, they would do. It so happened that their means of financial gain was by taking it, which they enjoyed over any other way. As the Range Rover's horn continued blowing, Teflon slid back and passed Treacherous the additional helmet. Treacherous got up out of the area before the police arrived, knowing it was just a matter of time.

As usual they had come off for the day. Not only did they get the New York kid for an expensive, thick platinum chain, which they learned was valued at 40,000 dollars due to the iced-out Jesus piece on it, a platinum bracelet iced-out, and an iced-out Cartier watch, combined valued at another 25,000, they also lifted 7 Gs in cash that Teflon had taken out of the kid's pockets. "Come here."

"What?" Teflon seductively cooed, walking toward him.

"You know what, take all of that off."

"You take all that off," Teflon shot back, pointing her finger up and down at Treacherous's clothing. They went through this all the time; each one fighting for dominance in the bedroom. "You heard what I said. Take that shit off," he repeated.

He and Teflon always became turned on after successfully pulling off a caper.

"And you heard what I said, take that shit off," Teflon returned. She then leaned in and grabbed two fistfuls of Treacherous's T-shirt, then kissed him. Treacherous knew what was coming next and he didn't try to stop it. As she passionately kissed Treacherous, Teflon, all in one motion, tore his shirt off him, exposing his bare chest. "You're crazy," he said, moaning. This was the third shirt that week Teflon had ripped off his back. Teflon jerked at Treacherous's belt.

"And take these off 'fore I rip 'em too." Treacherous laughed to himself. He unloosened his belt, unbuttoned his jeans, and let them fall to the floor while Teflon ran her tongue all over his chest. Teflon made her way back up and continued with her lip lock. He hiked Teflon up in the air and stepped out of his jeans. She wrapped her legs around his waist as he guided her to the bed. Still in a lip embrace, Treacherous laid Teflon onto the bed. He exchanged her lips with her breasts. She moaned. Her nipples were sensitive, especially when they were in Treacherous's mouth. Treacherous reached between her legs and grabbed hold of her thong. As he continued to sex Teflon's breasts with his tongue, he tugged on her thong and snapped it. Teflon jerked behind the sudden rip. Treacherous had never ripped anything off her before, but unbeknown to her, he had been waiting for the opportunity to pay her back for the many shirts, wife beaters, and boxers she had torn off him. It turned Teflon on to feel the fabric sliding between the crack of her anus and slit of her sex as Treacherous removed it from between her inner thighs, replacing it with his mouth. He buried his face between her legs and attacked Teflon's clit with expertise. He had been going down on her nearly every night and had become a master of the art. Within seconds he had Teflon's juices flowing and pouring into his mouth. She pushed his face deeper inside her as she rotated her hips. She held onto his head and sexed his face. Back-to back-Teflon climaxed again and again. Treacherous broke free of Teflon's lock and removed his boxers. He climbed onto the bed ready to join in on the pleasure.

"No," Teflon stopped him. "From the back." She moaned. Before she could turn over Treacherous flipped her onto her stomach. She arched her back and cocked her ass up in the air. He guided himself inside her and grabbed hold of her waist. He used her waist to pull her toward him with each thrust. Teflon rammed her ass into him as he pounded her sex box. The sounds of her juices enhanced as his flesh slapped against hers.

"Ooh yeah, right there, harder," she sang. Treacherous continued pounding, clenching his buttocks for harder thrusts. He was driving her crazy. "Spread my ass," she commanded and he complied. "Umph," she said as he slammed all ten inches of himself inside her wetness. The sounds of the headboard knocking up against the wall was in sync with his pumps. "This is your pussy," she told him. "This my dick?" she then asked.

"Yeah, this ya dick, babe," he growled. "This all yours," Treacherous added, increasing his pace.

"Smack my ass."

Treacherous instantly complied. The sound of his hand smacking Teflon on the ass echoed in the air.

"Harder," she cooed.

"Ooh yeah, daddy." Teflon could feel yet another orgasm coming down as Treacherous delivered the second smack to her right ass cheek.

"Put your finger in my ass."

Treacherous raised up and massaged his thumb into her ass as he shortened his strokes. She began to wind her hips, feeling his thumb penetrate her anus. Treacherous replaced his thumb with his middle finger. Teflon raised up on all fours. She began backing into him. He slid his middle finger in and out of her ass while he continued to sex her. She looked back at him. "I want you to cum for me. Make that dick cum for me."

That was all it took for him. He removed his finger from inside of her and spread her cheeks for a second time. He watched as his dick slid in and out of her, sliding it nearly all the way out, leaving just the tip of the head inside her, then deep thrusting back in. Moments later, he couldn't withstand the sensation that overcame him. Teflon knew when he was reaching that point. She worked her hips like magic.

"Aagh," he yelled out as she continued to gyrate her hips into him until he was drained.

He lay on top of her, forcing her body to the bed. Just like many of nights after a good job was pulled off and great sex, that was the way they had fallen asleep.

Chapter Fifteen

Normally it would be just like any other Sunday, a laid-back, cool-out type of day for both Treacherous and Teflon, but this was no ordinary Sunday. This was a day that would determine how they would live for the rest of their lives. Treacherous had thought long and hard about the matter and had to put a lot of time and planning into his thoughts; as much as he could without alerting Teflon of his intent, slipping away from her every chance he got to map out what it was he had been working on, which was not an easy thing to do. For many years Teflon had been his shadow and he had been hers. He knew she would never question his whereabouts whenever he dipped off, but she had to have wondered why she was not invited, or even told where Treach was sliding off to. In due time, he promised himself to tell her just as soon as he obtained enough information and was sure what he intended for them to do could in fact be done by just the two of them. The times when he would step out, he made sure to stick a couple of cats up in the process of making it home just to reassure Teflon he was not out in the streets disrespecting her by stepping outside of their relationship to creep with the next chick.

Since the first time they made love, Treacherous had never had another urge or desire to be with any other woman but Teflon. To him, she was more than enough woman, both inside and outside of the bedroom. Though she satisfied him to the fullest sexually, their relationship went far deeper than that. Over the years they had established an unbreakable bond from their youth up until now. Teflon was not only his girlfriend and lover, she was his companion, his best friend, his better half, and even his codefendant. Overall, Treacherous felt Teflon was his soul mate. He thought back to how after that first day of them being together, him being a free man, he had come straight out and told her he had only been with one other female besides her when he was thirteen, and how it happened, word for word. He was not ashamed or embarrassed behind the story. He told it with confidence, but not with praise or glorifying it, and Teflon respected him for sharing his past with her. She told him that the stripper may have been his first when he was still only a kid, but she would be his first and only with him as a man, and since then she had proven that to be true. Treacherous shared everything about his past with Teflon and in return she did the same, even her own sexual past; how the foster-care providers (the men) tried to molest her and she took to the streets for survival and how she had only been with one other man prior to him, and Treacherous had believed her. He told himself even if she had been with a hundred men, it would not change the way he felt or thought about her, and he knew that after him, there would be no other.

It was about 6:10 in the morning when Treacherous woke up, somewhat disturbed out of his sleep by the thoughts that filled his mind. He began to replay them in his head, and thinking back on him and Teflon's history aroused him. Beside him lay Teflon, her beautiful brown body nude with one arm positioned on her forehead as if she was posing for an art class. What more could a man ask for in a woman? he thought as he admired her beauty. She looked so at peace as she slept that his manhood began to stiffen. Laying on her back revealed her best physical assets, beginning with her voluptuous, smooth-looking, mouthful-sized breasts that stood firm, along with her flat, ironing-board midsection that contained a light trail of hair running from her navel down to her neatly trimmed bush, which invaded her inner thighs. She still possessed her little waist, but over the years of good living and good loving, her hips had spread out, giving her an hourglass-shaped body. The way she lay on the bed, he could see a great deal of her backside from the front, but any man who knew about voluptuous bottoms knew that Teflon was holding. What turned Treacherous on the most about his lover were her pretty, self-manicured feet. For some reason he had a real big foot fetish and loved to wash, massage, kiss, lick, and suck on Teflon's toes. He recalled watching a movie with her one day when Eddie Murphy would check the feet of the women he had sexed by sliding the covers off them while they were asleep, and Treacherous would say to Teflon that's what kept them together for so long, because if she in fact had busted wheels their relationship would not be as strong. Teflon would laugh and play-fight with him, but Treacherous was dead serious.

By now he was as horny as a brother who was up in a strip club after doing twenty years, but Teflon seemed so at peace as she slept he did not want to wake her just because he wanted to be pleased, especially when he was well capable of pleasing himself. He used to pleasure himself to thoughts of Teflon when he was up in the youth house, which he later told her about, so he didn't see any reason why he couldn't do it again in the privacy of his own home while she lay there in the flesh. Treacherous snatched up the K-Y jelly they kept on the nightstand and began to masturbate next to Teflon with one hand, placing his other between her legs. He closed his eyes and imagined his own hand as Teflon's.

Teflon began to moan in her sleep as she felt something between her inner thighs. Unconsciously, she began slow grinding with Treacherous's rhythm of what was between her legs. She felt something inside of her, but just couldn't bring herself to open her eyes to see what it was. She thought she was dreaming and didn't want to ruin the dream. She had never had a dream that felt so good. Had she not felt the tingle that began to take over her body, she would have continued to believe it was a dream, but she knew better. When she opened her eyes and looked over, she saw what Treacherous was doing.

Treacherous's eyes were closed. He had not realized Teflon had awakened. He was so caught up in the rapture that at that point nothing else mattered besides his releasing his load. As he stroked, he felt Teflon's inner thighs moisten and he knew he had brought her to a climax by playing with her clit, and the thought sent him into overdrive. His strokes went from long and slow to short and fast as he felt himself building up, ready to explode. As his orgasm reached the middle of his erection, he started breathing heavily. As he moaned Teflon's name he began to twitch and jerk, as that familiar tingle overpowered him, but he intended to ride this wave all the way and let his juices flow where they landed. As he began to explode his hand was replaced with something warm.

Teflon lay there watching Treacherous as he continued to play inside of her warmth. As she watched him and made love to his fingers, she was turned on and got off. Treacherous told her how he used to masturbate to thoughts of her when they were younger, and she was pleased to have been that thought, but she had never seen him in the actual act before. She believed she had provided him with enough sex to prevent him from having to result to such tactics, but seeing her man jerk off while he played in her kitty kat had Teflon on fire like she had never been before. She didn't even know such a feeling existed. The more she watched, the more she learned about Treacherous. She watched how he handled himself gently but with a sense of firmness and made a mental note of it for the next time when she would give him a hand job. She compared the way Treacherous masturbated to the way she had pleased herself and realized that just as a woman knows the right places and spots to touch to get the best results, men did also. Based on both his movements, Teflon knew her man was reaching his peak. He switched from slow, long strokes to short, fast ones, breathing heavily. He called out her name. It was seeing and hearing that that caused Teflon to spring into action. If it was her who he thought about pleasing him, then she was going to see to it that she did just that. Without him realizing it, Teflon slid off Treacherous's fingers, and in one motion, grabbed the hand he used to pleasure himself. She then swung her leg across Treacherous's frame and straddled him.

When Treacherous opened his eyes, he was surprised to see Teflon on top of him, but had no complaints. She was just in time to catch all of his love juices inside of her, he thought, as he adjusted himself up under Teflon for a better position. Teflon placed her hands on Treacherous's washboard abs and began to finish with her hips what he had started with his hand, taking him all the way inside of her before his semi–rock-hard muscle softened completely. She rode Treach the way a cowgirl rides a bucking bronco, with skill and expertise, not to mention passion, milking him of all his cream, until he went limp, and when it was all said and done, she sat on top of Treacherous and broke the silence.

"I couldn't let you just waste that like that," she jokingly said.

Treacherous looked at Teflon and grinned. "You shot out."

"That's why you love me."

"Says who?" he joked.

"Says you, nigga," Teflon shot back, attempting to hop off of him while delivering a punch to his chest. Treacherous caught Teflon by the hips, preventing her from getting up.

"Where you think you going?" Teflon remained silent.

"Cut the shit," Treacherous said, sensing Teflon's attitude. "You know I love your mu'fuckin' ass."

Teflon could not hold back her smile. "You better," she said, leaning down to give him a kiss.

"Get the fuck out of here," Treacherous replied, moving his head out of kissing range.

"I love you too, Treach."

"Go to sleep."

Chapter Sixteen

After the two of them had dozed off for what seemed like the entire evening, exhausted from what had just transpired, Treacherous sat up from the bed and began rubbing his head as if he were trying to gather his thoughts.

"Babe, what's wrong?" Teflon asked, concerned as she often was whenever he seemed troubled. She rose and slid closer to Treacherous, but he stood. Although he was a great lover to Teflon, he was not an affectionate man, and Teflon knew that. She felt the need to be up under her man, hoping it would have at least made a difference. When Treacherous was disturbed there was nothing anyone could do or say that could ease his disturbance, not even Teflon, and she was the closest thing to family since his father had been taken away. For years, Treacherous had dealt with and handled his problems on his own by thinking them out, and it was only after that he would share what had been troubling him with her.

"Tef, I been doin' a lot of thinking, boo," Treacherous started. Teflon could hear the conviction in his tone as she became more attentive. "I'm getting tired of robbin' these petty fake-ass ballas out here. I mean, the paper is sweet and it's easy money, but we ain't getting nowhere, though," he expressed with disgust. "We been doin' this shit together for more than ten years now, almost twelve including the youth house and ain't really got shit to show for it. Yeah, we got that little egg nest stashed for a rainy day and we ain't wanting for nothin', but we still livin' up in this crib, going out scopin' the same faces out here to run down on, and doin' just the same ol' shit. We ain't never even left up outta Virginia. Don't get me wrong, I love my hometown, but I'm tired of mu'fuckin' VA, and on the real this shit too small for us now. We bigger than all this, bigger than this whole fuckin' state, boo, word. That's why we gotta start thinkin' big, like them muthafuckas that come down from up north, from Philly, Jersey, and New York, and shit. As much as we keep robbin' them niggas, they still caked up 'cause they come down with that get-rich-or-die- trying attitude, that's how we gotta be on it."

As Teflon listened she felt where he was coming from even though she had no idea what triggered him, but whatever the reason, she was down for whatever. She was following Treacherous as he spoke, but missed what he was getting at.

"So you wanna start hustling?" she asked

"Nah, boo, never that. You know we ain't wit' that shit. We strictly about takin' these fools' paper, but our shit is a hustle too, so we been hustling. Shit is deeper than the drug game, the shit I'm talkin' about. I'm talkin' about some shit that will take us up outta mu'fuckin' VA. We'll be able to go anywhere we want to and just cool the fuck out, probably bounce down to Florida or something after this shit, cop a nice spot just off the beach. When I was in the youth house I used to read about how nice it was out there and Atlanta too. That's supposed to be the new black mecca of America for our people, like how New York supposed to be. We could chill out there; anywhere besides out here."

Teflon never heard Treacherous talk this way before. To be so young, they had been together for a long time, but to hear Treacherous speak about their future together and leaving Virginia sounded real appealing to her, and she knew she would do whatever it took to assist him in making his plans for the two of them to become a reality.

"Babe, you know I'm wit' you, a hundred percent on whatever you say, but what can we do besides what we already doin' to make all of that possible?" she asked.

This was the moment Treacherous had been waiting for—the moment of truth. He had been mapping out his plan for quite some time without Teflon's knowledge and felt he had it all figured out, and now it was time to share his plans with his better half.

"Straight up, we gonna knock off a bank," he told her, letting his words marinate inside her head as he watched her taking in what he had just dropped on her.

It took a second for it to compute before she realized what her man had just sprung on her.

What Treacherous had stated so boldly was not like any other job they had knocked off together. Their robbing spree only consisted of minor-league dudes from the streets who acted like heavyweights, but what Treacherous was talking about was in a league of its own. He was talking about stepping into the major league of the game where the real heavy hitters dwelled. She recalled the time when Treach had told her how his father had gotten cased up for hitting a bank and how he started out robbing just like them, but became a certified bank robber and was good at what he did until he took down the wrong bank by himself. Her mind raced a mile a minute. She wasn't afraid because to her a bank was no more dangerous than a street dude. Her thoughts were more focused on the bank plan itself. She knew it would take a great length of time to mastermind a plan to take down a spot as secure as a bank. Besides that, she was down for her man, so she wanted to hear the rest.

"Treach, you know that's not easy, right?"

"Boo, I know that, which is why I did my research, and believe me when I tell you, I did my muthafuckin' homework. I been casin' this joint out for almost a month now; daytime, afternoon, and night; just watching their whole operation inside and out, who's who and what's what, the slow days, the busy days, the time they open, the time they shut down. I even followed a couple of workers home. I peeped how they operate inside the bank and all of that, and I know where the little white muthafucka live that got the key to open the vault after he punch in the security code. Boo, trust me. I got it all mapped out. Now you know where I was at when I wasn't wit' you all those times, that's what I was doin', handlin' my business. You probably thought I was wit' some other chick, but you know I don't pump like that. It's me and you against the world, babe; Bonnie and Clyde, Romeo and Juliet, all wrapped up into one, but harder than all of them put together. After this shit, mu'fuckas and their bitches gonna be comparing themselves to Treacherous and Teflon."

Teflon smiled at Treacherous's analogy. He always made her feel like they could accomplish anything they put their minds to, so after hearing how thoroughly he had sought out and broke down his plans to her, she acquired that same familiar feeling he had instilled in her years ago. To her, this would just be another easy-ass job for them, no major difference than the others besides the fact that it would be their biggest one ever, but either way Teflon was in.

"A'ight, let's do this," she said to Treacherous, becoming more hyped behind the thought.

"That's my girl," he yelled.

"We about to come the fuck up. Me and you, boo. Me and you against the world."

"Me and you against the world," Teflon repeated.

"Okay. We gonna tie up a few loose ends, then as soon as we do this last move we gonna take down this bank."

"Whatever you wanna do, boo." No matter what, Teflon would ride with her lover. That's how it was and that's how it would always be, she believed.

Chapter Seventeen

For the next two weeks Treacherous and Teflon went on a massive robbery spree, accumulating as much valuables as they could in order to perfect their future plan, which they had been discussing intently each night before they took it down. During that time, all the hustlers and ballers alike were on full alert throughout the whole state of Virginia, because word had traveled at a rapid speed that Treacherous and Teflon were on a rampage. They went through the roughest hoods like they had license, and any and everybody who was out when they came through at the time felt their wrath. They were becoming such a nuisance in the Tidewater Park area that hustlers who had known Treacherous all of his life and had a great deal of respect for both him and his father were plotting to kill him and Teflon on sight wherever they caught the duo. Some were even taking it a step further by going out in search of Treacherous and Teflon in hopes of finding them. They knew if they succeeded, their street creditability would skyrocket.

Treacherous and Teflon went underground, patiently waiting to resurface for what would be their last petty street caper before they took down their big score.

Chapter Eighteen

The strip of Norfolk's Waterside Drive was body infested Memorial Day weekend. Some of the hottest whips and motorcycles in existence owned by the biggest hustlers from state to state flooded the side streets of Main and Martin Avenues, unable to get onto the strip due to it being blocked off for the festivities. Police were posted everywhere to ensure the Afram Festival kicked off. Snipers were even posted on roofs of buildings, anticipating the worst due to the masses of young black men and women dominating the crowd.

Like every year, many from the Virginia area traveled to Myrtle Beach in South Carolina for Bike Week to have a good time, but judging by the atmosphere of the Afram Fest crowd, many others felt this was the place for them to be, including Bricks and his motorcycle club, who drove all the way from Jersey to attend, lugging their bikes on trailers. Normally, Bricks would have been one of the first bikes on the scene at Myrtle Beach, but last year's event left a bad taste in his mouth, causing him to choose another part of the south to have a good time in. He had caught two homicides and could have nearly gone to jail behind an altercation he had on the strip with another hustler from New York who thought Bricks was trying to talk to his girl, not knowing it had been the other way around. Bricks despised New Yorkers because he felt they thought they were better than the hustlers where he was from, so rather than trying to explain that he had no interest in the New Yorker's girl, Bricks pretended to bow down, letting the hustler from New York blatantly and verbally disrespect him.

Unbeknown to the New York hustler, Bricks had been trailing him the entire night. When the timing was right, Bricks rolled up on the New Yorker and shot him twice in the face with his silencer-equipped Glock. Just as he was about to make his exit, Bricks noticed out of the corner of his eye that someone had spotted him. Before the young pretty girl who had seen too much could flee into seclusion, Bricks had planted two to the back of her head. Bricks was from Newark, New Jersey, aka the Bricks, but that wasn't where he had coined his street moniker from.

Bricks, whose real name was Tyrone Jenkins, earned his name in the streets from being known for the large masses of bricks of heroin he distributed throughout the tristate area, as well as the south. Not to mention the bricks of cash he was known for carrying in his pockets whenever he stepped out.

Bricks had a reputation for shutting a club down whenever he entered, buying out the bar. In strip clubs worldwide, women who had heard of him or had the pleasure of dancing for him or giving themselves to him for a generous fee, rushed to his presence when he and his entourage entered the building, knowing it would be beneficial at the end of the night. Rumor had it that in a strip club in South Plainfield, New Jersey, Bricks was so impressed and turned on by the dancers' performance on stage that he made it rain with ten grand, tossing a hundred 100-dollar bills onto the stage at the eight exotic dancers, taking five of them out the club with him for him and his four-man crew.

Bricks never left the house without at least 25 grand in his pockets, which is why his motorcycle club brothers, who were also a part of his drug team, stayed strapped at all times, just in case someone wanted to try Bricks.

It had been a long and eventful day and overall Bricks had enjoyed himself, especially the performance by old school rappers Slick Rick and Doug E. Fresh. The evening had wound down and now it was time to switch into chill mode. All Bricks wanted to do was take a shower to wash away the residue from today's heat, smoke a stick of the goodness he and his crew had brought with them, sip on some cognac, hit a club, and find a female or two he could jump off with for the rest of the night, if not the rest of the weekend. His suite with the adjoining room at the Sheraton was just right for him and his crew. Bricks was already contemplating sexing something young and tender on one of the two balconies the suite possessed. The suite's fridge was stocked with Coronas, and between the half pound of sour diesel weed they had, the four-gallon bottles of Hennessy, two fifths of Rémy, and the Smirnoff and Alizé they had for the ladies, it was guaranteed the after-party would be going down up in suite 774.

"Yo, pass me that stick, my dude," Bricks said to his man.

Once the professionally rolled blunt was in his possession, Bricks took deep and long pulls of the potent weed. "Yeah, this what I needed right here," he said, looking at the blunt as if he were admiring it. "Yo, y'all got everything? We gonna hit this club called Reign right up the street and around the corner."

They all knew what Bricks was asking. Everybody nodded, indicating they were strapped.

"Yo, we walkin' or ridin'?" Bricks's man, who had passed him the blunt, asked.

"Nah, I'm takin my baby with me, she too pretty to leave sittin' downstairs. I'm takin' her out," Bricks replied, making reference to his brand-new R1 motorcycle as it were a woman.

"You think we gonna be able to get in with the heat?" another of his manz questioned.

"Money talk, daddy, we good. When haven't we ever been able to?"

What Bricks said was gospel. They had never gone anywhere, regardless to what state, and had a problem getting in with their weapons. Even if Bricks had to slip the bouncer or doorman a thousand dollars, they always made it in a spot strapped.

"We out."

The line for Club Reign was wrapped around the corner when Bricks and his crew pulled up in front on their bikes. The sign read, WITH SNEAKERS 150 DOLLARS, WITHOUT 50 DOLLARS. None of them had on sneakers but knew their boots qualified them to pay the 150. Heads turned, seeing the expensive rides. Each bike had been tricked and piped out with the most expensive chrome and tires. Each body had a design that read *Brick City Ryders,* with their respective names on the side, but it was Bricks's bike that stood out among the five riders. His name was emblazoned in a wall of bricks with bricks of money stacked on top of the wall. Everywhere he went he saw to it he represented his street handle and made sure everyone knew who he was. He had been getting money in the dirty south off and on for a decade and a half, trafficking and transporting ounces and eventually kilos of cocaine throughout the Carolinas, but it wasn't until he cut into the heroin market in Virginia that Bricks started seeing major paper. Between Richmond and the seven cities of the Tidewater Park area, Bricks was stacking his paper by the bricks, distributing ounces of dope and thousands of bundles daily. Bricks couldn't help but grin as he scanned the club's waiting line, noticing a quick five females he had sexed a time or two. Each one tried to get his attention, hoping they would be able to enter the club with him, avoiding standing in the lengthy line, but Bricks pretended not to notice the women. Tonight, he wanted something new and fresh with a sexy face and the body to match.

"What up, Bricks?" one of the bouncers at the entrance greeted. Bricks recognized him from another club out in Virginia Beach he frequented whenever he came down to the dirty. He recalled how cool the bouncer was, and the fact that he was from his home state of Jersey, originally from Plainfield, made him remember the dude, not to mention the 500 he had slipped him to get inside with his twins and his crew and their hardware. Bricks knew it was too easy now to enter with their weapons. He slid his right hand into his front pocket and smoothly peeled off the first thirteen bills his hand came in contact with. Not that it mattered, because he only traveled with hundreds in his pockets. "Biggs, what's good, my dude? What it is?" Bricks returned, remembering the bouncer's nickname. As the two men embraced, Bricks slapped the thirteen crisp 100-dollar bills into Biggs's monstrous palms. The two men hugged as if they were old friends to make the scene seem genuine. The actual transaction had gone unnoticed.

"They're all with you?" Biggs asked.

"No doubt."

"That's what's up."

"Bricks," a female voice called from the crowded line, but Bricks ignored it.

The bouncer just smiled. "What's going on up top? I ain't been up there in a while."

"Same ol' shit, my dude. Young cats killin' off young cats. Nobody wanna eat anymore, smell me."

"That's crazy."

"Yo, Biggs, you want me to let the ladies in?" one of the other bouncers asked.

"Yeah, they good."

Bricks and his team admired the four young females wearing next to nothing as the bouncer held the entrance of the club's door open for them to strut on in.

"That's what it is," one of Bricks's boys was the first to say as he too made his way to the door. The others followed.

"Yo, I'll holla at you, my dude. Stay up and good lookin'," Bricks said.

"You too daddy." The two of them shook hands and embraced for a second time before parting. The doorman opened the door for Bricks to enter the hot spot. The sounds of T.I.'s latest cut poured out of the establishment and into the streets. Despite the loud music, as Bricks walked toward the entrance, his attention was drawn behind him by another familiar sound. Bricks stopped in his tracks and turned to see who had pulled up across the street on the Ducati. Surprisingly, although he could only see the eyes through the helmet shield, judging by the physical shape, Bricks knew the rider was a female. Instantly he was turned on. He possessed a Ducati, but what turned him on the most was not the bike but who was on it. "Yo, you know who that is?" Bricks doubled back and asked Biggs.

"Nah baby, never seen that bike up here before, but whoever it is, she stacked. I don't know what the face lookin' like but the body sure tight," Biggs answered, making the same observation Bricks had.

"Definitely," Bricks replied as he attempted to slide over to where the female rider was parked.

"Yo, B, what's really hood my dude?" one of Bricks's crew members called out to him from the doorway of the club. He had doubled back once they all had noticed that Bricks wasn't among them. They were all overprotective of him and at some point had to prove just how much love and loyalty they had for him, each man laying their life on the line, risking their freedom in the process, to show they had his back.

"I'm good, homie. I think I might be onto something. Let the homies know I'm good," Bricks called.

"You sure?"

Bricks didn't answer. Instead he shot him a look that told it all.

"That's what's up." The crew member knew not to take it any further. Everyone in their camp knew what the look meant. Bricks had a way of checking you without uttering a word.

Bricks continued to make his way across the street to where the mystery woman with the powerful bike sat. He had reached her just in time to take in her beauty as she lifted up her helmet and rested it on top of her head. He could see traces of blond hair spilling out of the sides of the helmet while he admired her baby-soft skin. Just what the doctor ordered, he thought. "Damn, sweetheart. No disrespect, but you gots to be the hottest chick in Virginia right now," Bricks complimented.

"Is that right?" she replied.

"True story, ma. You're serious."

She smiled.

"Nice bike too. I got one of these. This ya manz?"

"No. It's mine. And I don't have a man."

"Oh, okay. That's what's up. What's ya name, ma?"

"It ain't ma," she shot back with a slight attitude.

"No need to get hostile," joked Bricks. He had been through it a million times. He had a habit of calling females *ma* and always ran into some who had a problem with it.

"I'm not getting hostile." She smiled. "My name is Candy."

"Like caramel candy," Bricks slyly remarked, making reference to her skin tone.

"I guess."

"I'm Bricks." He held out his hand.

"Nice to meet you, Bricks," Candy replied, shaking his hand. "You from up north, huh?"

"No question, Jerze."

"One of those your bike over there?" Candy asked.

"Yeah, that's my baby over there," he proudly boasted, turning to point to the R1.

"That's hot. I always wanted to ride one of those. How do they ride?"

"Like a bronco. Might be too much for you."

"Huh, I can ride anything," Candy retorted. Something about the way she said the word *anything* caused the semi-bulge in Bricks's jeans to throb.

"Anything, huh?" he repeated.

"That's what I said."

"How would you like to go for a ride now?" Bricks offered, having more then just a ride on his R1 on his mind.

"I'm game."

"That's what it is then. Hold up."

Bricks pulled out his cell phone. "Yo, can you hear me?" he asked, the chirp breakin' up. "Yo, if you can hear me, I'm out. Catch y'all back at the spot."

Bricks placed his phone back in his hip clip. "Where you wanna go?" he asked.

"It don't matter," Candy replied.

"Well, let me ask you another question. Where you don't wanna go?"

"It don't matter," she repeated.

"There it is then, follow me." Bricks glanced at his ice bezel. It was 1:30 in the morning. He would have to catch the club another time, he thought. Tonight he was going straight to the after-party.

"A'ight playboy, I see ya work," Biggs called out as Bricks hopped on his bike. Bricks threw up the peace sign then peeled off.

Candy started up the Ducati, revved the engine, and followed suit. Bricks made his way back onto Waterside Drive, headed toward the Sheraton. He decided to skip the ride he'd offered to Candy on his R1 for now and take her back to his hotel suite for what he felt would be the ride of her life. Bricks put on his right blinker to turn into the valet parking of the hotel, but Candy flew right pass him, blew her horn, and waved for Bricks to follow. Bricks detoured and took pursuit as Candy flew up the ramp of Exit 9 and merged onto Highway 264.

Bricks's speedometer read 120 miles per hour as he played catch-up with Candy. He was turned on by how well Candy handled her bike. He was used to females being the backseat passengers, but Candy rode like a pro. Bricks increased his speed, pulling close to her rear tire. His speedometer read 140 miles per hour now as they zoomed through the open highway of 264 East.

Just as Bricks was about to become parallel with Candy, he noticed out of his periphery that another bike had joined them on the highway. Caring less about the unwanted addition, Bricks continued to increase his speed. He and Candy were now riding side by side. Bricks saw that Candy began to break her speed down now that he had caught up to her and he did the same. They were now doing a comfortable 80 miles per hour. Again, Bricks noticed the other rider off to his right, pulling up alongside of him As he pulled up, for a split second something inside of Bricks began to feel uneasy. Despite his panic button going off, Bricks brushed off the notion.

Treacherous pulled off the ramp of Exit 11 seeing the two bikes ride by. He had been waiting for the past hour for them to cross his path. Treacherous gunned his R1 down the highway in an attempt to catch the two power-ful motorcycles. Having his R1 upgraded, it was easy for him to catch up. He was a speed demon, so it was nothing for him to push it to 160 miles per hour. He had mastered the art of riding and feared nothing. When Treacherous reached the back of the rider on the R1 he deliberately fell back until he was fully ready to execute his plan. He had been working on this caper ever since he had seen Bricks sorting out his money by his bike in the parking lot of Military Circle Mall. Treacherous had estimated at least 50 to 80 grand in Bricks's hand. Treacherous had just passed another rider with a knapsack on his bag and assumed the two men had just made a drug transaction. Treacherous was tempted to get Bricks then, but couldn't risk someone walking by and foiling the whole idea. See-ing the two bikes breaking down their speed, Treacherous reached into his shoulder strap and sped up.

A second too late, Bricks saw the black-nozzled hand-gun that was now drawn on him by the biker. Though he had two himself in his possession, he knew reaching for one could cost him his life. His other option was to make a run for it and let the chips fall where they may, but that idea was x-ed out when he saw out the corner of his left periphery that the female rider had moved in closer to him. When he looked, he couldn't believe the chick Candy also had a gun pointed at him.

Teflon was pleased with how easy it was for her to manipulate Bricks to leave with her. She and Treacherous had already discussed the possibility of her having to single-handedly rob Bricks in the vicinity of the club if Treacherous couldn't infiltrate the area. She knew she was capable of pulling it off, but she preferred the plan to be followed through by the both of them. They were a team, and she was used to doing things as one. Teflon knew Treacherous wanted this last vic badly before they moved on to bigger and better things, and she wanted things to go in accordance. Once Teflon saw Treacherous had joined the scene, she slowed down so he could pull up. She had seen Treacherous draw his weapon even before Bricks knew someone had gotten the drop on him. Teflon also drew her weapon. She sensed that Bricks was contemplating his options so she moved in closer to let him know they were limited. Teflon imagined the look on Bricks's face underneath his helmet once he realized the fix was in.

The facial expressions of all the men she had put in compromising positions with her beauty always amused her. With the exception of Treacherous, she had never met a man who wasn't sex driven. She didn't believe all men were, just the ones she came in contact with who ran the streets. Coming up on another exit, Teflon waved her gun for Bricks to get off. Treacherous was already veering off with his gun focused on Bricks. Teflon pointed hers at his back tire in case he tried to make a mad dash for it. Bricks had no choice but to comply. He was steaming inside. He couldn't believe he had been caught with his pants down so easily. He wanted so badly to make a run for it, but he was no dummy. He knew the odds of getting away were slim. The deck was stacked against him, and Bricks knew he had to respect the rules and charge this one to the game.

Treacherous was the first one off his bike once they lead Bricks to the secluded area. Teflon hopped off her bike and snatched the keys from Brickss' bike ignition.

"You got me, bitch," Bricks mumbled from under his helmet just enough for Teflon to hear as she drew close.

Teflon smiled. "Your mama," she shot back.

"You know what's up, chump," Treacherous announced now, walkin' up on Bricks.

"A. Empty your pockets, B. Die trying to be a superhero and have your family pull out their best black suits."

Bricks snickered at the corny robbery speech. *Mu'fucka probably rehearsed that shit a million times,* Bricks thought. In his younger years he had been robbed by some killers. The ones who did talk let you know they meant business. Bricks didn't believe the two who had gotten the drop on him were from that same bloodline. The more he thought about it, the more trying them became appealing to him. "Ain't no C option?" Bricks asked sarcastically.

"Nah, just A and B, clown." *Boom.* The thunderous roar echoed in the air as the hot slug tore into Bricks's chest. He gasped. The shot came out of nowhere and caught him by surprise. He had underestimated the gunman totally, he realized and it had cost him.

"Babe, when I pull him off the bike, go in this fool's pockets so we can get up out of here. We'll come back for the bike 'cause where he goin' he ain't gonna need it," Bricks heard Treacherous say. Bricks did not want to believe this was his final fate. Back home many would have tried to murder him in the blink of an eye if they knew he had access to a million- three back home in hopes of obtaining his hood riches. Now here he only had a little over 40,000 dollars and was sitting on his motorcycle bleeding to death. Not because he didn't want to give up the money he possessed, because he had plenty of it, but because his ego overpowered his intellect and his mouth wrote a check that bounced. Bricks saw Treacherous raise his gun. He closed his eyes and prepared himself for life after death. Treacherous planted two more slugs into Bricks's chest plate, then snatched him off the bike. "Go ahead, babe. I'ma stash the bike until we come back. We'll dump the body before we go."

"Alright."

Once everything was taken care of Treacherous and Teflon went back underground until the time had come for them to take down what they considered their final job.

Chapter Nineteen

It was officially judgment day that separated the men from the boys, the women from the little girls, the gangstas from the lames, big-timers from the small-timers, those who were ahead of the game from those who were late, and the strong from the weak. This was it, the moment of truth; it was either now or never and for Teflon and Treacherous. They had come too far to turn back now, there was no looking back.

"Boo, you double-checked those other whips?" asked Treacherous, pulling alongside Teflon in the CLS to get the getaway cars they had stashed.

Treacherous had come up with a plan that any notorious bank robber could be proud of. He intended for him and Teflon to drive together until they came across another vehicle that would be useful in their upcoming plan, then separately drive to the bank. Once they succeeded in their attempt to knock off the bank, the plan was to ride off from the job, again separately, taking two different getaway routes, which they had mapped out thoroughly, stashing two additional whips positioned along the route as a means of diversion in case someone spotted the initial vehicles. The Benz Treacherous drove had been obtained that morning right before they reached the bank from two unlucky wannabes who were just at the wrong place at the wrong time, or rather the right time depending on who it came from. Treacherous reflected on the carjacking he and Teflon had just committed nearly an hour ago and felt no remorse about the extent of the results. It was nothing personal because he didn't even know the two dudes, it was just business. They had something he needed, so he took it and to assure that his major objective wasn't foiled they had to go, it was just that simple. He and Teflon had far too much blood on their hands to be worrying about two nobodies now. Their only concern was the bank, which sat ten blocks up from where they pulled over to talk. Treacherous knew Teflon had secured all areas because the night before they had gone over everything one last time, including scoping out the bank the whole day. He was only doing a final security check just as an extra precaution, and Teflon knew that.

"Yeah, I left them unlocked, and the keys are in the sun visor. We good on that," replied Teflon.

"Cool. It's almost seven-thirty. Yo, I'ma meet you inside, a'ight?" Treacherous said, looking at his watch.

"Um-hmm," Teflon responded, doing the same, knowing that their watches were synchronized.

"Let's do this then," Treacherous said to her right before he began hitting the power-window switch, rolling the CLS window back up.

Chapter Twenty

Like any other normal day, the middle-aged white bank manager proceeded to unlock the front door of the bank for the employees to come in and set up their teller stations before the bank was officially opened at 9;00 a.m. The sixteen employees, which included ten bank tellers, five secretaries, and the assistant manager, all waited until 7:00 to arrive like clockwork for the bank manager to let them inside, each employee anxious to start their Monday morning. As each watch either beeped on the hour or the hands struck seven, everyone noticed the bank manager approaching the door. He disarmed the alarm using his specially made key, which was the actual kill switch.

As the door opened, the employees began entering the establishment. "Good morning," he greeted his colleagues one by one without looking up as they piled into the bank while he secured the door with the stopper. This was something he ritually did every day. Just as he secured the door the final employee stepped inside. He counted sixteen pairs of shoes while he was bent down. Nine women and seven men, and now it was time to lock the door until opening time. He knew it would have been easier to just hold the door open for everyone, but with him nothing was that simple.

As the bank manager began to rise, he noticed another pair of shoes that stopped directly in front of him, only they weren't really shoes, they were construction boots.

Timberlands, he recognized. Instantly a sense of fear overcame the bank manager as his panic alarm went off inside
of him. Seeing the tree symbol on the side of the boots, the
bank manager knew that whoever stood over him was not
an employee, because in his ten years as a bank manager
he never saw any employee wear a pair of Timberland
boots to work. He wondered if anybody else had seen the
unknown person who stood over him, because he was too
afraid to look up. All the other employees were so busy
trying to get situated no one even noticed what was taking
place by the front door. There was no doubt in the bank
manager's mind that if he looked up he wouldn't like what
he saw. Before he could decide what he was going to do,
the decision was made for him.

Treacherous pulled up a few feet away from the line of
people he knew were employees standing in front of the
bank, waiting to be let in. He had watched and timed the
same scenario for weeks so he was already familiar with
the drill. It was five minutes to seven when he pulled
up. That gave him more than enough time to check his
weapons. Treacherous knew the bank manager wouldn't
open the bank door until 7:00; not a minute earlier or a
minute later.

By the time Treacherous's watch reached one minute
to seven, he was exiting the CLS. He had timed how long
it took for him to get out of the vehicle and walk at a normal pace to the bank, bringing him to the estimated time
for the manager to unlock the door. Just as he thought,
the employees were all so caught up in getting inside
to prepare for the early-morning rush that his presence
went unnoticed as he saw the first twelve employees enter
the bank. Just as the last one walked through the door,
Treacherous was only a foot away. He pretended to be a

passerby on his way to work. *So far, so good,* he thought, seeing as how none of the employees bothered to even look back. Treacherous had seen the bank manager struggle with the door stopper many times and knew that the manager's struggles would be a key factor and beneficial to him when it came to getting inside the bank. Treacherous saw the manager had finished securing the door, only to have to unsecure it and lock it back. He laughed at the white manager's daily routine, thinking how easy it would be to just hold the door open himself, but when it came to white people they always made the simplest things seem like such a difficult task, Treacherous thought. Because of that, Treach intended to capitalize off his ridiculous, complicated method.

Treacherous had both of his weapons out as he walked through the door before the manager had time to close it. He stopped directly over the kneeling man, waiting for him to rise as he scanned the bank to see what the rest of the employees were doing. Everyone was off doing their thing, preparing themselves for the 9:00 rush, which was a good thing for Treacherous. He knew he and Teflon would be long gone by then. When Treacherous saw the manager was trying to get up, he sprung into action.

"Don't be no hero, my man," he semi-whispered to the bank manager, placing the barrel of one of the cannons he possessed up against the manager's right temple. Without even looking back he could tell that Teflon had entered the building as well.

Teflon pulled up a few feet away from the stolen CLS Treacherous drove, just as Treacherous had started toward the bank. It was 6:59 with 20 seconds until the hour when she looked at her watch. She checked her .380 and Beretta while she waited for the last of the employees and Treacherous to enter the bank. Once she saw Treacherous enter, she tucked her two burners and exited the Chrysler

Crossfire, leaving the doors unlocked. She took a quick glance around as she walked toward the bank. When she reached the front door she could see Treacherous standing over the white bank manager with his two pieces out inside the bank's entry. As she came through the door, she walked right up on Treacherous kicking the man to the floor, causing him to land flat on his back, and she too immediately went into action.

Chapter Twenty-one

"Ohmigod!"

Hearing the young white girl scream caused the rest of the employees to stop in their tracks. When they all looked up they saw Treacherous standing there with two monstrous guns pointed in their direction, one to the right side of the room and the other to the left. Before anyone could really react, Treacherous and Teflon were already on top of things and had all perimeters secured.

"Everyone put their mu'fuckin' hands up and come out here where I can see you," Treacherous demanded as Teflon secured the front door of the bank, locking the safety lock, which didn't require a key. That was something they had noticed while doing their homework on the bank.

Treacherous had counted the bodies as the employees appeared in plain view and began lying on the bank's floor.

"I know it's sixteen of you mu'fuckas in here not including your boss, and I only counted fifteen, so whoever is missing better show their face before you be responsible for all the dead bodies out here," he yelled.

Hearing that, one of the women tellers immediately spoke up.

"He's in the bathroom. I'll go get him," she said through sobs as she attempted to head toward the bathroom.

"Bitch, who told you to move?" barked Teflon, running up on her and throwing her to the ground by her blond hair.

"Babe, go get that nigga the fuck up outta there," Treacherous instructed.

"Y'all better hope that nigga ain't got no cell phone up in there, 'cause if he do, y'all some dead asses."

Less than a minute later, Teflon was escorting the young kid out of the bathroom. Treacherous couldn't help but laugh inside, seeing the conditions of the young white kid; his khaki pants still to his knees, a *Playboy* magazine, and an iPod in one hand while he rubbed his head with the other. Throughout all the commotion going on inside the bank, the kid had no clue what was going on. The only thing he knew was he had been cut short of his bowel movement and now stood in front of a group of people with his shriveled-up penis exposed and an un-wiped ass. He had never been so embarrassed in his life, but he was not only embarrassed, he was also in fear of his life because he had just been pistol- whipped by a woman who he knew meant business.

"Get your white ass over there," Teflon told the kid while pushing him toward the others.

The boy tripped on his own pants, feeling more embarrassed, but got back up and pulled his boxers and pants up. The smell of feces began to reek.

Now that they could account for all seventeen bodies, Treacherous felt more in control of things.

"Now check this out, nobody has to get hurt as long as the gentleman right here cooperates," he said to the fearful audience, grabbing the manager's arm in an attempt to help him up off the floor.

"Don't nobody try to be no mu'fuckin' superheroes and think they faster than a speeding bullet. Remember, this is not your money. The bank is insured. Think about making it home to your family in one piece before you try something stupid. Babe, hold it down while I handle this," Treacherous said to Teflon.

"Go ahead, boo, I got this," she replied.

"Let's go, my man," Treacherous said to the bank manager, escorting him to the vault.

Teflon held her guns on the sixteen employees as Treacherous and the manager slid off. Although she didn't want any casualties, she wouldn't hesitate to murder any of the hostages who made a false move.

Treacherous and the manager reached the back of the bank where the vault was located.

"Check this out, I'm going to make it easy for you so you don't have to try to lie and cause your family to get all dressed up and make funeral arrangements. I know that you got the key to this piece and know the security code to this vault. Now you get one chance to open this piece, and if I detect any funny shit that's your ass! You understand?" asked Treacherous.

"Y—y—y—Yes s—s—sir," the manager managed to reply nervously.

"Well, handle your business."

Treacherous had the two army duffel bags out waiting for the manager to open the vault. He watched carefully as the manager punched in the bank vault code, making sure nothing seemed out of the ordinary, but even by looking he really had no way of knowing. Once he punched the last number in and it computed, the manager stuck the special key in the vault's keyhole and turned it.

Treacherous heard the *click* and chalked it up as being the sound the vault key made when it was unlocked.

The bank manager seemed extremely nervous as he began opening the bank's vault. When he turned the handle and pulled the vault door open, Treacherous's dream had become a reality right before his very eyes. It was if he had died and gone to heaven. There was money everywhere stacked up wall-to-wall. One would have thought they had just been shown the official money-manufacturing room for the world, there was so much paper in there. Wasting no time, Treacherous planted one of the duffel bags in the manager's chest.

"Fill this up, and you bet' not try to give me none of that money with the dye packs on them either," advised Treacherous as the manager looked at him, surprised.

"Yeah, you ain't think a nigga like me knew about that, huh? I ain't as dumb as you think I look. Load that shit up," he ordered the manager.

Once Treacherous saw the bank manager begin filling up the bag with bulks of money, he began to fill up the other one. Within a few minutes both bags were full.

"Carry that back out front." As the manager toted the heavy bag, Treacherous followed him.

Teflon, as well as the hostages, were relieved to see Treacherous and the manager reappear. They had been in the bank for little over half an hour, which was longer than they anticipated and now it was time to wrap things up and make their exit.

"Babe, get this bag," yelled Treacherous, pointing to the duffel bag the manager struggled with.

Teflon went over and took the bag from the manager. She was strong for a woman, so the bag didn't even faze her when she put the straps around her shoulders and hiked it up to wear it like a backpack. Treacherous had already secured his bag, so there were only two more things left for him to do. Teflon had done her part by having all the hostages tied up and gagged, so he only had to have the manager done the same way while he went to get the security tapes out of the main office.

"Babe, tie his punk ass up while I go get the security tapes."

"Okay and hurry up."

"Yeah."

Teflon noticed the look of disgust on the bank manager's face when she turned in his direction.

"Wipe that shitty look off your face," Teflon barked, smacking the manager in the face with her Beretta.

The bank manager yelled in agony as blood gushed out of his nose.

"Bring your ass over here," she ordered, grabbing the manager by the arm. All the other employees began to whimper and murmur. They were actually more afraid of Teflon then Treacherous. By the time Teflon had tied the manager up, Treacherous had the eight security tapes—the four regulars and the four backup ones to be on the safe side—and now it was time to roll.

Treacherous noticed the manager holding his nose and that a new color was added to his once brand-new pants. He looked at Teflon. She shrugged. All he could do was shake his head.

"We appreciate your cooperation. Luckily we ain't have to kill one of you nice people. Just sit tight; someone will find you, eventually," Treacherous said with a little humor in his tone.

Chapter Twenty-two

After making his final remark, Treacherous and Teflon attempted to exit the building. It was ten to eight when Treacherous unlocked the door. As soon as he opened it, he stuck his head out slightly as an extra precaution before walking out of the bank, headed toward the CLS with Teflon not too far behind, making her way to the Chrysler.

Treacherous reached the Mercedes and opened the passenger-side door, throwing the duffel bag in the backseat and closed the door back, then proceeded to the driver's side.

Just as he opened the driver's door he heard the sound of his partner's voice simultaneously with the shots.

"Treach!" yelled Teflon as she pointed her .380 and 9 mm Beretta in the direction of the police and began squeezing the triggers.

Turning around, Treacherous noticed the large amount of police cars and police and quickly joined Teflon.

"Babe, get in!" Treacherous yelled over to Teflon, attempting to cover her as police returned fire.

Treacherous saw Teflon was now only shooting one gun while holding her side with the other.

At the sight of that Treacherous went ballistic.

"Boo, get in the car," he yelled again as he continued to fire.

Teflon struggled to make her way into the CLS, just barely escaping as a bullet shot out the passenger window just as she opened the door. She leaned over and put the duffel bag in the backseat, then started the Benz up with the key Treacherous had left in the ignition.

Hearing the Mercedes engine start, Treacherous let off two more rounds, then hopped in the car and sped off. Bullets continued to rattle the vehicle as Treacherous burned rubber. He had emptied all but one bullet in the two sixteen-shot 9's he had and replaced them with the two revolvers he had under the seat. He wondered how he and Teflon had been ambushed.

Chapter Twenty-three

"Excuse me, sir," the switchboard operator of the special security service said to the man behind the desk.

"What is it, Debbie?" he asked, somewhat agitated about being disturbed while smoking one of his favorite Cubans.

"I thought you should know that the silence alarm switch we installed at Bank of America on Waterside was just activated."

"What?" the security chief yelled, jumping up with cigar in hand. "When?"

"It just came in at seven-thirty."

He looked at his watch.

"That was three minutes ago. Okay, alert all local and federal authorities and let them know to meet our people downtown," he said as he put on his jacket.

"Yes sir."

As they sat there tied up and gagged, the bank manager sat on the floor, smiling, while the others still were in a world of fear, considering the possibility the bank robbers would want to come back and kill them all because they all had seen their faces. Only the manager knew they would never be coming back—not for a long time, anyway. It was just a matter of time before the cavalry came once they saw that the bank vault's silent alarm had been triggered. There was no way the inexperienced bank robbers could have known he had to put the vault key in first before he punched in the vault's code or else the silent alarm would be set off. The Bank of America had not had a false alarm with their system in many years, which was the last time they had been robbed. The robber had somehow managed to get into the vault and stayed in there overnight, constantly triggering the alarm, causing the main system to assume there was a minor glitch in the installment, after checking out the bank numerous times throughout the night. When the bank manager came in that morning and opened the vault, the robbers shot him and fled the scene. Not since then had there been any complications or false alarms with the system. The bank manager sat and waited patiently to be rescued and hear the final outcome of the bank robbers' inevitable fate.

Chapter Twenty-four

Treacherous continued to elude the police as he sped down the busy downtown street, running red lights and the whole nine, while Teflon sat across from him bleeding. He bucked a right on Garley Avenue, which was a part of his getaway route, wanting to get off the main strip. As he came up on Monticello he made a quick left, noticing one of the getaway cars he and Teflon had stashed on the corner. Had everything gone according to plan, he would have switched whips right there and kept going until he reached his second stash whip and doubled back to jump on the highway, but instead he had to change his plans and cut back sooner, busting a U-turn on Tazewell, which landed him right back on Waterside Drive.

Treacherous had made a complete 360 and wound up right back where he had initially begun. The police, who were in pursuit, thought they had Treach running scared and going in circles, until it had dawned on them he intended to take Waterside Drive all the way to the highway.

Treacherous gunned the black CLS, pushing the pedal to the floor as he entered onto the ramp, jumping on Highway 264 West, never slowing down. Within seconds the speedometer reached over 140 miles per hour. Treacherous noticed the helicopter overhead as he drove, but didn't pay them any mind. He was more focused on Teflon's well-being across from him.

Chapter Twenty-five

"Aye yo, Gunz, what's your last name again?" asked one of Richie Gunz's fellow inmates.

"Freeman, why, what's up? Six ball side pocket," replied Rich, taking his next shot on the pool table.

"Yo, you know some kid name Treacherous Freeman?"

Hearing his son's name caused Rich to pause mid-shot.

"What? Where did you hear that name at?" he wanted to know.

"Right here on the TV."

All in one motion Rich threw the pool stick down and walked toward the television. As he approached the day-room TV, he could see the newscaster Julie Sanchez on the screen, but he couldn't make out what she was saying.

"Yo, turn that up!" yelled Rich to one of the inmates who stood closest to the television.

". . . . Police authorities continue to pursue the two suspects, who seem as if they have no intentions on giving up at this time. We'll keep you updated as this tragic story continues to unfold here on Highway 264. This is Julie Sanchez, live from WAVY Ten. Back to you Bob."

"Thanks, Julie. Keep us posted. In other news, two teens were gunned down in the parking lot of a local McDonald's on Princess Ann Boulevard."

Rich missed the broadcast and wondered if it could have possibly been his son who the reporter spoke about. He hadn't heard from his son in more than ten years, since their first and last visit together, when he was in Lewisburg

Penitentiary, but he had heard about how Treacherous
had made and established a name for himself out there in
the streets. He blamed himself for the path Treacherous
had chosen because he became what Rich had raised him
to be. From what was told to him, his son was a bona fide
gangsta.

"Yo, what they say about the kid?" Rich asked the
inmate who asked him his last name, figuring he would
know.

"They say he and some girl from up out of Chesapeake
robbed some bank or something out on Waterside Drive
in Norfolk. I think it was Bank of America downtown. He
supposed to had shot three cops tryin'a get away and the
shorty with him got hit. They been chasin' 'em for over
an hour now. That's all they really said. Why, you know
him?"

"Yeah, I know him," replied Rich.

"I figured you did. I heard of him but I don't know him.
You know I been down longer than you so he wasn't makin' no noise when I was home. My cousin Charlie Moon
from Jersey that be out in Roanoke regulatin' mentioned
his name before; how the dude was gangsta with his out
there. Moon gangsta too, so for him to big the kid up he
gotta be about something. Is he any kin to you?" asked
the inmate.

"Yeah." Rich paused. "That's my son."

"Oh shit, dawg, I ain't know, damn!"

Just then the anchorman appeared back on the screen.

"Yo, hold it down," Rich said, raising his voice over
the noisy dayroom, motioning his hands for silence. He
was highly respected in the Petersburg medium custody
facility in North Carolina by some of the toughest dudes
from all over the world, so to ask such a request was not
asking for much. Everyone knew Rich didn't raise his
voice for anything unless he really had to. All who knew

him assisted him in quieting the dayroom. Everyone began to gather around the TV to see what held brother's attention.

The words *Breaking News* crossed the screen as the anchorman began to speak.

"This just came in. Our sources have found out that the black Mercedes-Benz CLS that police had been in pursuit of just hours ago had been reported stolen earlier today. It has now been confirmed that the CLS 600 Mercedes belonged to a Marcus Bullock of Brooklyn, New York. Mr. Bullock and another teen were gunned down in front of a local McDonald's on Princess Ann Boulevard, after being carjacked by Mr. Freeman and Ms. Jackson. The local authorities have confirmed the connection between the McDonald's murders and the bank robbery. Our sources also tell us that Mr. Freeman's father, a Mr. Richard Robinson, was convicted over seventeen years ago for single-handedly robbing the same bank for over a million dollars. He is currently serving a thirty-year sentence in Petersburg Federal Institution."

Everyone in the dayroom turned and looked at Rich, who continued watching the TV.

"Although this hasn't been confirmed, it is believed to be true that Mr. Freeman and Ms. Jackson took close to two million dollars. Hold on, I've just been told there has been some new developments in our top story. Julie, are you there?"

"Yeah, Bob, as you can see, the pursuit has come to an end. Police have the entire highway shut down. After reaching the Virginia Beach exit, the SUV stopped shortly thereafter on the ramp. Our sources tell us that Mr. Free-man and Ms. Jackson were ordered to throw out their weapons along with the vehicle keys, and they complied. We've also been told the officer in charge instructed the occupants to exit the vehicle. Apparently this is what authorities are waiting for—to take the suspects into custody. Hold on—the driver door just opened. Oh my god!"

Chapter Twenty-six

Treacherous laughed to himself at the naiveness of the officer.

Dumb mu'fucka, all that training for nothing, Treacherous thought, referring to how easy it was to fool the agent. He had snatched up the two P-90 submachine guns, with the see-through fifty-round clips on each side of the guns, which contained armor-piercing bullets.

He took one last look over at Teflon, then leaned in and gave her a kiss on the lips. They were still warm, Treacherous thought.

"I love you, Tef," were his last words to his soul mate before he grabbed the handle of the Benz with the intent of joining her.

He cocked the two submachine guns back and took a deep breath. He was not afraid to die. He knew that this was an option, but he never thought it would come down to this. The last time he was caught by police with guns on him it cost him five-and-a-half years of his life. He made a promise to himself he would never let them catch him like that ever again and now he vowed to stick to his guns, literally.

"Okay Treach, it's showtime, baby," he began hyping himself up. "This is for Teflon and your pops, and for all the gangstas who thought about holding court in the

streets. This is where it ends. Today is judgment day. Fuck a jury, let's rock!" He opened the CLS door.

The head agent in charge saw the SUV door come open and noticed a leg come out of the truck. All the sharpshooters, SWAT, and other officers became on full alert.

"Everybody stand down," yelled the head agent as Treacherous began to appear.

There were two things that caught the head agent's attention about the scene. One, Treach's hands were not on top of his head; and two, he could not see his hands at all.

"Mr. Freeman, put your hands on top of your head where I can see them, and turn around slowly and get on your knees!" he shouted through his bullhorn.

Treacherous began turning around but he disregarded the head agent's last request and he did not put his hands on his head.

"Mr. Freeman, I repeat—put your hands on your head!" he shouted again.

Hearing the head agent's request again, everyone began tightening their grip on their weapons. Just then they all saw Treacherous beginning to raise his hands as he continued to turn around, but by the time they realized he wasn't actually complying, Treacherous already had the drop on them.

Rich stood there with his arms folded in front of the TV as the rest of the dayroom watched along with him.

"As you can see, one of the suspects has opened fire on the authorities. It appears to be Mr. Freeman who is the actual gunman. There has been no sign of Ms. Jackson, but Mr. Freeman continues to attack authorities, as they are under rapid fire. I can't believe this is actually happening. For those of you who have just tuned in, this is live coverage of the shootout between one of the alleged bank robbers of Bank of America and the authorities.

Wait! Something seems to be happening. Police are running toward the Mercedes."

Treacherous raised his hands in an attempt to fake the officers out. When he spun around in plain view he wasted no time. Treachrous let off the two P-90s like Sylvester Stallone in *Rambo*. He had caught the police off guard and used it to his advantage. As he continued to spit fire in succession at the crowd he noticed several officers falling down like dominoes, while others tried to take cover. He intended to hold the triggers until each gun was empty, but his plans changed when he felt the first couple of bullets tear into his chest. The shots came out of nowhere, Treacherous thought, as he tried to keep his balance, but more followed the others, ripping through his left shoulder and lower torso, planting him up against the CLS, causing him to drop one of the P-90s. Treacherous's adrenaline was pumping so much you would've thought he was high off the purest cocaine sold. He was not on his feet but his finger still remained on the trigger of the other P-90.

The sound of shots was all Treacherous could hear until death knocked at his door.

The shot of the sharpshooter caught him right between the eyes. Treacherous's lifeless body slid down the side of the CLS 600 as the other P-90 fell to the ground. The remaining authorities then carefully rushed toward the Benz.

Rich watched all the commotion in the background and knew even before they announced it what had taken place. He held back his tears as the reporter spoke. He had not shed a tear since the last time he had seen his son.

"It's been confirmed this disastrous incident has ended in tragedy. Six state police and four federal agents were killed in the line of fire, five others were wounded. Mr. Treacherous Freeman was shot and killed during the horrendous shoot. Miraculously, Ms. Teflon Jackson was found unconscious with a bullet-inflicted wound inside the vehicle, but our sources say she is not expected to make it. The money was recovered inside of the Mercedes. What drove a young man to such a tragic ending, no one knows but that man himself. This is Julie Sanchez, live from WAVY TV Ten."

"Yo, turn that down for a minute," Rich told his man in front of him as he heard the murmurs and side conversation from the men behind him, each man congregating with who they deal with about how his son had gone out like a trouper, or how they would've handled it if it were them, or how they were going to do it the same way if they ever got caught again; each man caught up in his own fantasy world, but not having the slightest indication or clue about what really took place on the idiot box, which Rich referred to the TV as. Before he left the dayroom he intended to take them to school and educate them on the reality of the matter.

"Yo, check this out, right," he started. "I hear all you brothers who think you gangstas, killas, thugs, or whatever you consider yourself to be, talkin' about how my boy went all out and how you would've handled it if it was you out there. It's funny to me because if that's how you would've gone out, if it was you, then you wouldn't be up in here talking about it." He was now upset and his emotions began to kick in. "A lot of you brothers had the chance and opportunity to let the streets decide your fate, but you chose to pick twelve or took a plea instead of being carried by six, but my son chose the latter. That was all he knew because he was raised like that. I raised him to be that way and now because of that, my biggest fear and worst nightmare has become a reality, and I fault myself. I don't know if you brothers are fathers or not, but I know you got little brothers, cousins, and nephews who look up to you and probably want to be just like you when they grow up, so just know that whatever you do when you get up outta here, those little brothers that look up to you will be trying to imitate you, so if you with destroying our youth and our generation, then do you, and if you really think you built like that to hold court in the streets, then remember this day because the same way we all stood here watching my son, some of us will be in this very same dayroom watching you, 'cause that's how it goes down!" ended Rich, leaving every man in the dayroom in deep thought.

Some listened, while others let it go in one ear and out the other, but no matter what they chose to do with what Rich said, they all had heard him and had to respect his words because he was just keeping it real.

Chapter Twenty-seven

Her vision was blurry as she opened her eyes. She had been under heavy observation for the past four days, expected not to survive. It had been a crucial and life-threatening four days, but being the strong individual she was, she had survived, although she felt a little weak. She had no clue as to where she was, not even aware that she was unconscious for a period of time. Upon gaining some of her sight, she began trying to focus on where she actually was. She attempted to wipe her heavy eyelids, feeling the coal on them that made it difficult to clear her vision, but came up with a short hand, now realizing she had been handcuffed to something.

With her free hand she wiped her eyes and as her vision became clearer she noticed she had been handcuffed to a hospital bed. But that was not all. She had a tube stuck in her chained-up arm, which ran from a machine and she saw another one running from a machine up under her hospital gown. For the life of her she couldn't figure out how she wound up in a hospital, cuffed to a bed, and why. Her memory was a blur, and she had no recollection of what had taken place days ago. She began moving only to find out her whole, entire body was sore. But why? She had no clue.

She continued looking around, searching for clues that would give her some indication how she was in the predicament she was in. As she looked to her left she spotted a newspaper on the hospital nightstand next to the bed. She painfully reached over and grabbed the paper. The date read October 28, and she couldn't determine whether the newspaper was actually that day's or yesterday's because she had no knowledge as to what day it really was. The front page had a headline that stuck out to her, but she didn't know why. It read in big, bold letters, Bonnie and Clyde of the New Millennium. Up under the heading was a picture of a black CLS. Even before she began reading the article, the photo of the car triggered something inside her as images of it began to fill her mind, causing her to remember some things. Within the first four lines tears began to roll down her face. Reading her soul mate's name caused Teflon to regain all of her senses and have her thoughts restored. Everything all made sense now. October 28 was the day they decided to rob the bank; the headline referred to her and Treacherous; the Mercedes was the car she and Treach had jacked and murdered the two young dealers for to use on the bank job; she had taken a shot to the side as they were coming out of the bank, and Treach had taken the police on the high-speed chase in an attempt to get her to the hospital, which was all she could remember. As she continued to read, the rest was answered for her in black-and- white, how Treach had gone all out right there on the Virginia Beach exit while she lay there unconscious.

Teflon's tears flowed harder as she envisioned the scene. She knew there was only one thing that no one else could know besides her, what would make Treacherous take the route he took. The only thing that would have made her take the same route had the situation been different and she was in his shoes: If the other thought the one was dead. How could Treacherous have thought she was dead? she wondered. Was her pulse or heartbeat that low that it went undetected? Teflon wanted to know the answers to those questions because they were the answers that caused her to lose her other half; or her better half, as Treacherous would say. She smiled at the thought. She remembered when Treacherous had first told her about the bank and how he had said that after that day every nigga and chick would be comparing themselves to Treacherous and Teflon. He had said they were like Bonnie and Clyde and Romeo and Juliet all wrapped up in one, but harder, and everything he said was coming to pass. Teflon herself had viewed their love for each other as a Romeo and Juliet relationship because they too were young and in love, and just as Romeo took his own life, assuming Juliet had been dead, Treacherous had basically done the same, and just as Juliet woke only to find out that Romeo was dead, so did Teflon.

She began beating herself up, knowing had she not been unconscious she and Treacherous would have gone out together in a blaze of glory. She began ripping the tubes from up out of her in an attempt to find a way to take her own life, just as Juliet did, so she could meet up with her soul mate again.

While she was in the process of doing all of this, the doctor walked in, catching Teflon in the act and rushing over to her.

"Ms. Jackson!" the doctor yelled, grabbing her free hand.

"Calm down. You're all right. You and the baby are going to be fine. Just take it easy."

Up until his last statement Teflon continued to resist the doctor's attempts to restrain her, but hearing what he just said registered enough to get her to instantly stop what she was trying to do.

"What did you just say?" she asked the doctor, making sure she had heard him correctly, as she cleared her throat.

"I said to take it easy, you and the baby are going to be fine," he repeated.

Right then Teflon noticed the officer, who she assumed stood guard by her room door, stick his head inside.

"Is everything all right, doc?" the white, young-looking officer asked, hearing all the commotion from the hallway.

"Yes, everything is fine," the doctor replied, not wanting to cause a scene or get the pretty young girl in any more trouble than she was already in.

By now, Teflon had calmed down completely after getting the doctor's confirmation on his last statement.

"That's better," expressed the doctor as he started reattaching the tubes that Teflon had snatched out of her.

"It's good to see you awake. We thought we were going to lose you, but you're a strong young woman."

Teflon watched him as his hand slid under the hospital blanket with the intent of reconnecting the tube that was once stuck in her side. She felt his hand brush up against her bare hips and flinched. No other man had touched her body in over twelve years besides Treacherous and the thought of the doctor's foreign hand on her brought chills through her body.

"I got it," she said, moving the doctor's hand.

"Oh, I'm sorry," said the doctor, thinking he had hurt her. "Are you sore?"

"Yeah, a little."

"All right. I'll see to it that you get something to help with the pain and for infections as well. You took a nasty hit. It was iffy in the operating room."

"How long was I unconscious?" Teflon asked.

"Four days."

"Damn. What about the baby? How long have I been pregnant?" she asked.

"You mean you didn't know?" the doctor asked, surprised.

"If I did I wouldn't have asked," replied Teflon with attitude, becoming agitated.

The doctor caught the hostility mixed with sarcasm and blamed it on Teflon's condition.

"You're five weeks pregnant."

Teflon thought back to the last time she and Treacherous had made love and began to smile at the thought, as tears streamed down her face once again. Their last encounter was the time she had awoke only to find Treacherous masturbating with one hand while he had his other one between her thighs. She remembered all too well and realized that had she not replaced his hand with her love box that day, she would not have a part of him growing inside of her. Adding this new piece to the equation caused Teflon to rethink her plans. There was nothing else she wanted more in life than to join Treacherous, wherever he was, whether it be heaven or hell, but because of the five-week-old life that dwelled inside of her, her plans to meet up with her better half would have to be delayed and their reunion would have to be put on hold; at least for another eight months.

ORDER FORM
URBAN BOOKS, LLC
97 N18th Street
Wyandanch, NY 11798

Name (please print):_____

Address: _____

City/State: _____

Zip: _____

QTY	TITLES	PRICE

Shipping and handling: add $3.50 for 1st book, then $1.75 for each additional book.
Please send a check payable to:
Urban Books, LLC
Please allow 4-6 weeks for delivery

ORDER FORM
URBAN BOOKS, LLC
97 N18th Street
Wyandanch, NY 11798

Name (please print):_____

Address: _____

City/State: _____

Zip: _____

QTY	TITLES	PRICE
	16 On The Block	$14.95
	A Girl From Flint	$14.95
	A Pimp's Life	$14.95
	Baltimore Chronicles	$14.95
	Baltimore Chronicles 2	$14.95
	Betrayal	$14.95
	Black Diamond	$14.95
	Black Diamond 2	$14.95
	Black Friday	$14.95
	Both Sides Of The Fence	$14.95
	Both Sides Of The Fence 2	$14.95
	California Connection	$14.95

Shipping and handling-add $3.50 for 1st book, then $1.75 for each additional book.
Please send a check payable to:
   Urban Books, LLC
Please allow 4-6 weeks for delivery

ORDER FORM
URBAN BOOKS, LLC
97 N18th Street
Wyandanch, NY 11798

Name (please print): _____

Address: _____

City/State: _____

Zip: _____

QTY	TITLES	PRICE
	California Connection 2	$14.95
	Cheesecake And Teardrops	$14.95
	Congratulations	$14.95
	Crazy In Love	$14.95
	Cyber Case	$14.95
	Denim Diaries	$14.95
	Diary Of A Mad First Lady	$14.95
	Diary Of A Stalker	$14.95
	Diary Of A Street Diva	$14.95
	Diary Of A Young Girl	$14.95
	Dirty Money	$14.95
	Dirty To The Grave	$14.95

Shipping and handling-add $3.50 for 1st book, then $1.75 for each additional book.

Please send a check payable to:
Urban Books, LLC
Please allow 4-6 weeks for delivery

ORDER FORM
URBAN BOOKS, LLC
97 N18th Street
Wyandanch, NY 11798

Name (please print):_____

Address: _____

City/State: _____

Zip: _____

QTY	TITLES	PRICE
	Gunz And Roses	$14.95
	Happily Ever Now	$14.95
	Hell Has No Fury	$14.95
	Hush	$14.95
	If It Isn't love	$14.95
	Kiss Kiss Bang Bang	$14.95
	Last Breath	$14.95
	Little Black Girl Lost	$14.95
	Little Black Girl Lost 2	$14.95
	Little Black Girl Lost 3	$14.95
	Little Black Girl Lost 4	$14.95
	Little Black Girl Lost 5	$14.95

Shipping and handling-add $3.50 for 1st book, then $1.75 for each additional book.
Please send a check payable to:
Urban Books, LLC
Please allow 4-6 weeks for delivery

ORDER FORM
URBAN BOOKS, LLC
97 N18th Street
Wyandanch, NY 11798

Name (please print):_____

Address: _____

City/State: _____

Zip: _____

QTY	TITLES	PRICE
	Loving Dasia	$14.95
	Material Girl	$14.95
	Moth To A Flame	$14.95
	Mr. High Maintenance	$14.95
	My Little Secret	$14.95
	Naughty	$14.95
	Naughty 2	$14.95
	Naughty 3	$14.95
	Queen Bee	$14.95
	Say It Ain't So	$14.95
	Snapped	$14.95
	Snow White	$14.95

Shipping and handling-add $3.50 for 1st book, then $1.75 for each additional book.

Please send a check payable to:
    Urban Books, LLC

Please allow 4-6 weeks for delivery